A BREED APART

A BREED APART

TONY GERMAN

An M&S Paperback from
McClelland & Stewart Inc.
The Canadian Publishers

An M&S Paperback from McClelland & Stewart Inc.

Copyright © 1985 by Tony German

Reprinted 1989

Canadian Cataloguing in Publication Data

German, Tony, 1924-
  A breed apart

ISBN 0-7710-3266-8

I. Title.

PS8563.E76B73   1985   JC813'.54   C85-098323-1

Cover illustration by Alan Daniel

Typography by The Literary Service,
Toronto, Ontario

Printed and bound in Canada
by Webcom Limited

McClelland & Stewart Inc.
The Canadian Publishers
481 University Avenue
Toronto M5G 2E9

*To Sarah and Pat, Sue and Greg and Dan —
good companions, who canoed the Missinippe
and shared with me its ageless beauty
and its power.*

Also by Tony German

Tom Penny (1977)

River Race (1979)

Tom Penny and the Grand Canal (1982)

Contents

1   Race for Home   *9*

2   Ile-à-la-Crosse   *27*

3   Nancy Spence   *44*

4   Harry Whistler   *59*

5   Wolverine   *71*

6   The New Year   *79*

7   Sunday Morning   *95*

8   Death on the Ice   *107*

9   Traitor   *118*

10   Exile   *135*

11   Spring   *142*

12   Lac la Ronge   *154*

13   Fall   *164*

14   The Hunt   *172*

15   Medicine Rapid   *185*

16   Winter   *190*

17   Fort William   *202*

18   Montreal   *213*

19   Chez le Boeuf   *223*

20   Rue Saint-Louis   *234*

21   On Trial   *242*

22   A Breed Apart   *258*

Glossary   *267*

1
Race for Home

"It's a rough game, laddies, I'll tell ye that. And it's a harsh land and a hard life, this fur trade." The firelight gleamed in Fergus Macdonald's fierce eyes and carved the lines in his face even deeper. Sixty years ago, Duncan Cameron thought, the old wolf would have been swinging a claymore alongside Bonnie Prince Charlie — just for the love of the fighting.

"But it's a man's life and ye're young. So take your pleasures where ye may. Hah! And your profits too. . . . And I'll gi'e ye a toast, gentlemen." He raised his mug to the glowing faces around the fire, then to the dim humps of the overturned canoes and the half-seen gleam of the Shagwenaw Rapid.

"Here's to the fur trade, and our canoes and our lakes and rivers and our voyageurs, and our sweethearts and wives. And here's to us. And. . . to hell wi' the Hudson's Bay." He tossed back his rum as though it was water and let out his long, full bellow of a laugh. Everyone joined in the toast — and the laugh. You had to with Fergus Macdonald.

"Well, I'm for my tent and my featherbed, gentlemen." He stood and stretched to his sinewy height. "Ye'll start the race at four in the morning, Angus Cameron? Aye. And here's five guineas that says my Athabasca brigade will leave your canoes standing still."

Duncan looked across the flames at his father. He was nodding, with that suspicion of a smile which seemed about as close as Angus Cameron ever came to a laugh. He was a stern man, unbending. But then Duncan hardly knew him. They'd only seen each other three times in the last ten years, until this two-thousand-mile journey by canoe from Fort William. They had travelled together for two months, but still it seemed they'd scarcely met. And tomorrow they'd be at Ile-à-la-Crosse.

The others he knew a bit better. Benson and Balfour were senior clerks and old hands at the fur trade. Gavin Farquhar over there was a sixteen-year-old greenhorn clerk like him. They'd met in Montreal, though they weren't close. Duncan Cameron didn't make friends easily. Then there was the hulking Wee Willie MacGillivray. He was green too, but with a silver spoon in his mouth. He wouldn't stay long in the northwest — not with his family connections. His uncle was the controlling partner in the whole of the North West Company.

Wee Willie. That took him back. So did the

sound of the rapid. So did the sliver of sky he could see through the tent flap when he had rolled into his blanket, with the stars and the pale-washed flickering of the northern lights. The last time he had lain here by the Shagwenaw, under the same stars and sky, with the same smell of wood smoke and the scratch of a blanket on his face, he had silently sobbed the night away. Ten years back. . . .

He was six years old then, a sturdy little brown-skinned boy, and his father was taking him to something he called 'school' in a distant place named Montreal. It was the nearest school there was, and the son of a gentleman of the fur trade must go there so he'd be like his father. But Duncan was afraid. Oh, he'd travelled in canoes before. He'd slept beneath them, unworried by the night noises and the wolves. He'd carried his share at the portages, been wet and cold and eaten by the flies. He'd moved from post to post with his family in the vast northwest — Reindeer Lake, Fort Chipewyan, Ile-à-la-Crosse — and every journey a new adventure.

Tents, makeshift cabins, comfortable houses, high-walled forts. They had once stayed with his grandfather and grandmother. Their smoky teepee dwelt in his mind as a magical place of warmth and love and wondrous tales. But this time his mother, whose name was Rose Flower, and his brother and tiny sister stayed behind. Where they were was home. And he had never left home before. Could he ever, in this endless land, find it once again?

The hollow ache he'd felt deep inside his chest receded during their three-month journey to Lachine. He was a favourite with the canoemen. Cadieux, the guide, saw in him his father's strong jaw with the cleft in the chin, his wide forehead and direct gaze. That small nose would one day be as prominent as his father's, Cadieux had said, and already there was a little of the Cameron purpose in his stride. There was also something of Madame, his mother, was there not? He had her full lips and generous mouth, darkly shining eyes, high cheekbones and, of course, the blackness of her hair and the colour of her skin.

They spoiled him. When his father gave stern instructions that he must carry his own pack, he was tossed on top of a voyageur's gigantic load and pick-a-backed over, pack and all. The avant in his canoe — the one who guided it in the bow — carved him a miniature paddle, held him securely between his knees and laughed wildly with him through the plunging rapids. He shared his father's tent and special food, but he was welcomed at the canoemen's fires to listen to their songs and their horrendous tales.

Lachine at last, then Montreal with the small boy's wonderment of riding by calêche, of paved streets and vast stone houses, tailors' shops and shoemakers, a thousand belching chimneys, clattering wagons, windmills and giant sailing ships. And then the desolate day when his father left him in his stiff new clothes in the attic dormitory at the school. The ache came back. The loss and the longing for his home. And something more.

It was waiting for him during the break in the first baffling morning of lessons. He set his wary foot outside in the yard, where the boys from the schoolroom stood in a silent ring. Waiting. Like a small animal he sensed the danger, and more than anything he wanted to run inside and hide. But he faced them. For a long time he simply stood his ground and faced them. And they didn't make a sound.

Then he just walked towards them with his hands out, palms up, as he would have done at home. He said, "I'm Duncan Cameron. . ." And they howled.

They howled at him and they circled him so he had no way out. They shouted and they laughed and jeered. They mimicked the difference in his speech. They pushed him around and around, hurled him from one to the next, flung him back and forth.

Twisted savage faces. Wolves tearing at a crippled caribou. Their shouting changed, picked up a taunting measured schoolboy chant. On and on it went, taking shape in words that battered at his ears, sunk into his mind, lashed him to his soul.

> *"Duncan Cameron, we can see,*
> *Your father is a Scotsman,*
> *Your mother is a Cree. . . .*

Half-breed, half-breed, one-two-three,
Your father is a Scotsman,
Your mother is a Cree. . . ."

He felt their blind contempt. He began to understand what lay behind their scorn.

They pushed their champion into the middle. He was big. Red haired and white faced, pudgy and slow on his feet. "Wee Willie. Go get him, Wee Willie. Go. . ." Duncan fought Wee Willie toe to toe and he bloodied his nose and made him cry, then he fought the rest until the school bell rang. They drew back, silent, and left him battered, blood-streaked and alone. Alone in the empty yard.

Sobs tore at his chest. They stored up and stored up inside, and no tears came to flush them out. There they stayed. And stayed. He was different. He knew that now. He was not like them. He was another breed — a breed apart.

"Are ye ready, lads?" Angus Cameron's voice stabbed across the water through the early-morning dark.

"Ready. Aye!"

"Bien oui, m'sieu!"

Shouts rolled back from ten great canoes fanned across the glassy lake. Duncan could see his father in the next one over — tall, erect, his beaver hat held high. He saw him throw his head back once again and he heard him roar, "Are ye ready, Athabasca brigade?"

From the dark came Macdonald's voice. "Ready? Aye, we're ready to trim ye, Angus Cameron. I'll gi'e ye a last chance to call off that wager noo."

Hoots and shouts backed up the taunt. They lay off to the right somewhere, the ten Athabasca canoes.

"Save your breath for the race, Mr. Macdonald, instead o' counting your chickens. Stand by, men! Attention, les gars!"

His pistol arm came up, up, up. . . .

Crash!

One shot. One mighty shout from a hundred throats, and a hundred paddles dug the water. Duncan's canoe leaped forward with the rest and they were off — all twenty of them — flying through the darkness, down the pond-smooth waters of Lac Ile-à-la-Crosse. Forty miles to go. Forty miles and they'd reach the fort. The last lap home — and flat out all the way.

The Athabascans, of course, had another three hundred miles to go. They were a swaggering lot. They claimed to be the toughest of them all, and they could be right. Once they'd raced another brigade two hundred and fifty miles up Lake Winnipeg non-stop, and won.

This time they'd overtaken Cameron's brigade in Knee Lake. They surged by, howling derision, then waited above Shagwenaw Rapid. Fire-eating Fergus Macdonald was willing to lose a couple of days out of his dash to reach Fort Chipewyan before freeze-up just to prove the Athabascans' claim in a forty-mile race.

Sixty strokes a minute. A bit better than that. Duncan felt the gunwale throbbing under his hand, a heartbeat that went on and on and on. They could do that for eighteen hours a day, those canoemen. More if they had to. And in a mere six hours they'd be home, at Ile-à-la-Crosse. And it was his home too, after all these years.

His hand fell on a spare paddle. Why not join in? It was a race, after all. And it would be dark for another hour. No. He settled into his comfortable place and pulled his blanket around his shoulders. Gentlemen did not paddle. Gentlemen got lifted ashore to keep their feet dry. Gentlemen did not become friends with canoemen, although they must understand them and look to their welfare — mainly to keep them strong, healthy and therefore working. Gentlemen. . . He'd heard so many things a gentleman did and did not do. No one had ever told him what a gentleman really was.

At sixteen, though, Duncan seemed to qualify — his father a full partner in the North West Company, school in Montreal, an apprenticeship in a good trading house. As well, he'd spent his holidays with the Letelliers. Raymond Letellier, Angus Cameron's wealthy partner, looked after the Montreal end of the business while Cameron spent his life in the Indian country bringing in the furs. Duncan expected to do the same, but not forever. Even though he'd been born here, this country seemed every bit as strange to him as Montreal had been when he was young.

The Letellier house had become his haven then. It was spacious, airy and light with laughter, and warm with crackling fires and spicy smells when he first went there at Christmas. Madame hugged him and instantly he loved her.

She said, "Duncan Cameron. Welcome. Call me Tante Angèle. Now, meet Gilles and little Marianne."

Marianne spun so her skirt flew, and showed off her curtsy. She ran off laughing and brought Duncan back an orange.

Gilles, his own age, appraised him through large brown eyes, rocking on his heels, his hands behind his back. Duncan returned his gaze until at last Gilles said, "I'll show you our horses. Will you show me how to be an Indian? Please?"

Duncan answered simply, "Yes," and they were friends.

He was part of the family on the holidays. He and Gilles got into endless scrapes. They had their battles, but mostly on the same side. When she got a little older, Marianne dogged their footsteps. At ten, they included her in their games because she had agility and spunk. At twelve, their world was for boys only and they went to endless lengths to lose her. Two years later she went away to school.

Since his first encounter in the schoolyard Duncan had been left strictly alone. No one really got to know him, and a myth grew that he, like all half-breeds, carried a concealed knife and would use it if provoked. He ignored the whispered barbs that he was really meant to hear. He stuck to his reading and his studies and his solitary rambles, and he lived for the end of school.

Three years into his apprenticeship at the company depôt at Lachine, he was invited, as always, to the Letelliers' springtime dance. As always, he had mixed feelings. He loved them and their house, but among the guests there would be some... Well, there was simply no avoiding that.

Fairy lights in the garden, carriages crunching up the drive. Cloaks, evening dress, red uniforms of officers. Candlelight and music in the hall, Wee Willie MacGillivray at the buffet table — as always — and Tante Angèle receiving guests. She was lively and warm and blonde-haired, overflowing almost from a splendid dress and glittering with jewels. She greeted him in French.

"Duncan, it's so good you're here." She kissed him and stood back, holding both his hands. "And how handsome you are, and so tall now. But too thin. We must fatten you up. And you should cut your hair shorter. It's the fashion for young gentlemen... Raymond, do look at his elegant tail coat and breeches. You must find out his tailor. And that fine shirt, and silver buckles on your shoes. You always buy so well, Duncan."

"Or borrow, unless we're paying our apprentices far too much these days," Raymond Letellier laughed. "He must have learned expensive tastes from you, my dear."

"Oh, pooh." She gave her husband's hand an affectionate pat and turned to her next guest.

"Welcome, Duncan." Letellier shook Duncan's hand warmly, then switched to English to speak to the elegantly dressed stranger beside him. "Mr. Southwell, may I present Mr. Duncan Cameron."

A quizzical nod, the head to one side, eyebrows slightly raised, taking in Duncan's distinctive features and his colour. No handshake offered. "Mr. Cameron." Emphasis on the 'mister,' a drawling English voice. "How very interesting."

"Mr. Cameron is one of the bright young gentlemen in our company. His father is my partner, away up at Ile-à-la-Crosse."

"Remarkable!" Southwell said nothing more. There was an awkward pause. Duncan moved on, barely hearing Southwell's lowered voice: "I say, Letellier, you fur trader chaps do have ah. . .a democratic way about you, what?" There was a hint of lewdness in his laugh.

Duncan stopped. That was enough. He turned back, his face tight. He could feel the flush rising in his cheeks. He swallowed hard, tried desperately to keep his words cool and even. "I think, sir, your notion of democracy concerns indulgence rather than equality."

Southwell jerked around. "I was not addressing you, my young friend. I. . ."

"Duncan Cameron!" It was Marianne Letellier. Vivacious, sparkling oval face, darkly flashing eyes. And grown. . . "Dance with me, Duncan. It's been so long."

"Marianne!" Breathless, he offered her his arm. She was stunningly, beautifully transformed. He turned back to bow briefly to the two gentlemen. A momentary frost clouded Raymond Letellier's eyes. Southwell's smile was cynical and cold. Duncan bowed to Marianne. She smiled at him, and he was lost.

Now, sitting in the canoe, he remembered it all so well, and smiled wryly to himself. Yes, technically he was a gentleman. But to be a true gentleman, being half white was not enough. Mr. Southwell was neither the first nor the last to make that view quite clear. Here in the northwest, though, it surely made no difference. Such things bothered these canoemen not one whit.

Like old Leo Bedard up there, the avant. Tiny. Wiry as a spruce root. "Hire the wee ones," Fergus Macdonald had told him. "They eat less, and they weigh less in the canoe so ye carry more goods up, more furs down. Economy, laddie, economy. Dinna forget!"

The two just ahead, moving in perfect time, were Silent Joseph — Jo, the Iroquois, with no last name — and Jacques Pinet. Usually Jo was next to naked, with a breech clout, moccasins and his silver Saint Joseph medal. This morning, though, he had on trousers and a clean white shirt. Ile-à-la-Crosse was home, though a long way from the place where he was born.

And Pinet — they called him Coco — always laughing, chattering, loud as a blue jay, prying into everyone's business. He outstripped the others in his boasting — shady deals, debauches, women left behind, feats of strength. He really could carry, though. Duncan had seen him running up past Kakabeka Falls with two packs on his back at ninety pounds each, and his fiddle case slapping at his side.

Of course a fiddler was always welcome. Favreau, the brigade guide, had engaged Coco as a replacement at Fort William. He couldn't find out much about him as a canoeman, but the fiddle turned the trick. He could play remarkably well, and he enlivened every camp. But he was as nimble at sidestepping work as he was with his fingers.

His canoemates agreeably carried Coco's packs up the long portage at Grand Rapid to allow him a lengthy prayer at one of the crosses there. He said it marked the drowning of his voyageur father. Then someone from another canoe said they'd seen Coco do the same at the Long Sault two years back, and another said it was at The Needle. Leo's crew couldn't decide whether they'd been hoodwinked by Coco or humbugged by the others.

The ice-bright stars were fading and the great black dome of sky was lightening around its lower edge to azure blue. Mist lay low across the water. It muffled sound and swallowed all but the nearest canoes. Duncan's mind slid back.

When they'd left Fort William the talk around the fires was all of the girls at Boucher's raffish tavern and the Ojibway encampment. Last night, though, they spoke of their own women and children at Ile-à-la-Crosse.

The gentlemen didn't join in the chat around the common canoemen's fires, of course. They had their own. But Duncan had memories too, which he kept to himself. . . . Saying good-bye to Marianne Letellier, for example. He could remember every tiny detail — the cool dimness of the emptied warehouse in Lachine, the noises of last-minute departure just the other side of that thick stone wall, the breathtaking slimness of her waist, his own clumsiness. . . . And then her whispered, "Au revoir, Duncan. Good-bye. Come back soon — please." And the warmth of her lips. Even though she'd pulled back with a teasing laugh, the wondrous feel of them was still there. Yes, oh yes. He would come back. With success and money of his own. To claim her and his place in business. And to show the world he could.

A voice broke out behind him. The first line of a paddling song. Ti'moine Tremblay, le gouvernail, the steersman, and the best songster in the whole brigade — some said in the whole northwest. Ti'moine struck up to the beat of his paddle.

"Ah, si mon moine voulait danser. . . ."

The whole crew echoed: *"Ah, si mon moine voulait danser."*

Ti'moine's favourite. About the girl enticing the monk to dance. Ti'moine — "Little Monk" was his nickname too — had never needed much enticement to dance.

Ti'moine again: *"Un capuchon je lui donnerais."*

Now every voice in the brigade picked it up:

"Danse mon moine, danse!

Tu n'entend pas la danse. . ."

The beat of the song and the beat of the paddles blended as they rushed on through the dawn.

"Danse mon moine, danse!" Montreal children singing in the streets, spinning their tops to the same old song. He could hear their piping chant. He could see them lash those tops with their thong whips to keep them going. *"Danse mon moine, danse!"*

Just as he had himself, long ago, in the house he could faintly remember at Ile-à-la-Crosse. His mother on the floor beside him, laughing and clapping, with the baby on her lap. The glow of a fire. His younger brother playing with the kitten. . . . That little boy had gone. Smallpox. Letters had told him of other children. Now Sally, Raymond and Catherine would be there to greet him, and perhaps to sing the song.

A child's song to go with a spinning top. A child's song to paddle by.

But this was no child's game.

23

The sun was high, striking autumn gold from the poplar-clad shore on either side. It had cleared the mist and it glanced off the mirrored surface out ahead. On the horizon was a distant smudge.

Duncan pulled his telescope from his pack and knelt, careful to keep the trim in the racing canoe. He focussed and the tiny white dots on the water took shape as gulls and pelicans. The smudge on the skyline, where the two shores seemed almost to converge, was a widespread haze of smoke. Beneath it. . .yes, a low shore, distant trees, and a straight-cut, ordered shape. A long palisade, bastions at either end. Above it a tiny square — the watchtower — and a dot against the sky. That would be the flag.

"Home in sight." He gave a shout. "Chez nous!"

"Yah!" Heads of paddlers flicked. The canoe answered with a sudden surge.

Duncan looked around at the others. They were moving very fast. Waves curled back smoothly from their high-built bows. Paddles moved like machines. There was not much in it. Fergus Macdonald was in the lead, with Angus Cameron close under his wake. The rest were strung out like a loose-formed skein of geese. Duncan reckoned his own canoe was about neck and neck with Balfour of the Athabascans. He had a side bet on with Balfour. Just a shade behind was Gavin Farquhar. They were doing well. Way back somewhere was the canoe with Wee Willie MacGillivray. His men had a dis-

24

advantage. He hadn't trimmed down over the years.

When they'd raced at Knee Lake, the Athabascans were riding lighter. That was usual because they had a good deal further to go before the freeze. This morning, though, with the heavy betting, the loads had been evened up as carefully as the weigh-in for a horse race.

He glanced back at Ti'moine, paddling as though his life depended on it. No time or breath for singing, though he could wink and crack a smile.

Now Duncan could count the teepees by the fort and spot canoes. Off to the right stood another fort, much smaller. That would be the Hudson's Bay's.

From the bastions leaped the sudden flash and puff of cannon. He counted, listening for the sound. . .seven seconds, eight, nine, ten. . . *Boom!*

"Two miles to go, you laggards! Now!" He saw Leo Bedard's head bob and his paddle move a fraction faster. The beat increased. Every paddle right together — faster, faster, faster. . .

Tiny figures were running to the shore. A crowd was growing there. The palisade gates were open. There was movement among the teepees.

A wolfish, whooping "Aie aie aie. . ." started in one of the canoes. It spread to all the rest. Duncan's voice cracked out the beat — on, on, on. For the last two miles they flew.

He saw his father's canoe pull up and pass Macdonald's. His own was close behind and edging Balfour's. "We can do it, yes, we can. Go, go, go. . ." One final spurt!

A cannon thundered for the winner, then another. Then one for Duncan's canoe and they were across the line. The paddles stopped. Canoemen flopped, their chests heaving, gulping air. The canoe slowed, slewed, drifted.

Shouts and cheers and barking dogs. A milling crowd along the shore.

They were home.

Ten years had passed and Duncan Cameron had come home.

2
Ile-à-la-Crosse

Duncan had conjured up a picture of his home-coming. Impeccable in his new grey suit and his tall beaver hat, he would be first to leap ashore. His mother would greet him fondly. She would be a laughing, full-figured Tante Angèle, but with straight black hair. They would embrace, speak easily to one another in the Cree he had been practising, and walk up to the house arm in arm.

He motioned to Ti'moine to paddle in, but he shook his head and pointed to Angus Cameron's canoe. There was ceremony to be observed. Le grand bourgeois, the gentleman in charge of the whole district, must be first to step onto the landing stage. Space on it was reserved for a special few. One gentleman waited stiffly, rigged in cutaway coat and breeches. That would be Peter Maclaren, in charge during Cameron's absence. He looked about thirty, square faced and rather pale. An Indian captain stood solemnly beside him, outlandish in his red coat, gleaming buttons and brooches, woollen trousers tied in at the knee, silver arm bands and tall decorated beaver hat.

"He is named Moose Runner," Ti'moine muttered, still breathing hard and deep. "He winters at Canoe Lake. That way." He pointed to the southwest. "Sometimes a good hunter. He changes like the wind, with the smell of rum."

There was a woman there too. She had three children at her side, and she stood tall and spare. Her face was strong, hawkish and deeply lined, and brown above the whiteness of her blouse. A paisley shawl was drawn around her shoulders and on it lay her braids of glossy black. She held an infant in a cradle-board. Her calf-length skirt was red plaid, crossed with lines of green, with beaded summer moccasins and leggings underneath.

This must be Angus Cameron's country wife, Rose Flower, the girl whom Cut Hand the Canoe-maker had given Crooked Nose Cameron eighteen years ago in a rich exchange of gifts. This must be Duncan's mother. He stared at her, hardly believing, groping to somehow span the years. His mother. Yes, it was.

Cameron was on the landing now. He shook hands with Peter Maclaren, turned to Moose Runner. They exchanged greetings formally in Cree, and there was a good deal more talk. Cameron presented him with a large silver bracelet. He received a fine pair of winter-caught cross-fox in return.

He turned at last to his wife, embraced her and the children. Then he took the new babe in his arms and kissed him. Favreau, the guide, raised his bull voice, calling for huzzahs for M'sieu le grand bourgeois and Madame and his whole family, and especially le petit. Angus Cameron raised the cradle-board high aloft. The voyageurs responded with three more mighty cheers.

Then Fergus Macdonald stepped ashore. Angus Cameron, his family around him, led his principal guest through the throng towards the gate in the great log palisade. Madame looked back as the crowd closed in. For him? Duncan failed to catch her eye.

Then there was a wild whoop from the canoes. Paddles thrust and they surged to shore. The crowd swarmed to surround them. Favreau's mighty voice drove them back, for the minute that it took to toss the packs ashore and lift out the canoes. Then there was a clamouring turmoil, of voyageurs and women, children and tots — leaping into one another's arms, kissing, laughing, dancing. Little ones were tossed up high. Youngsters dug excitedly in packs. Dogs barked and wagged and jumped.

Duncan found his own pack in the pile and the small cassette that held his valuables. He looked about for the other clerks, suddenly alone among this happy crowd.

There was Jo with a naked brown boy on his shoulders, a little girl around his knees. Old Leo had his arm around a pretty half-breed girl who could have been his daughter and who was showing him her baby with great pride. Ti'moine Tremblay was dancing in a ring with six children of varied age. A puppy frisked around their heels and a blanketed Cree woman watched and smiled and nursed her babe.

"Duncan Cameron?" A shy voice. He looked down into the bright brown eyes, the friendly, cheerful face.

"You *are* Duncan? Oh. . ." She bobbed a sudden curtsy. "I'm Sally."

"What a pretty girl you are!"

She looked about twelve years old, slight, lively, her head a little on one side, studying him.

"If you please, my mother says come to the house." She blushed, then curtsied again in a more possessed way, as though this time she'd planned it. She wore a Montreal print dress which was just a bit tight. Her English was stilted, with a slight lisp from her Cree mother tongue. Her voice, though, had a lilt, and she said "hoose" in the Scot's way.

"Come to the house? No, Miss Cameron." He shook his head.

"No?" Her eyes opened wide.

Surely this tall, dark young man in the smart grey suit *was* her brother. That dimple in his chin was like her father's, and he was certainly part Cree.

"No. I've come three thousand miles to see

you, and I'll not go one step further till I get a kiss." He dropped to his knees.

She paused, reluctant to warm too readily to a stranger. She clasped her hands in front in a quick gesture and stood for a moment. Then a sudden smile, and a step forward, and she kissed him on the cheek.

"Welcome, Duncan," she said. "Welcome home."

"Welcome to the house, Mr. Cameron." His father's greeting was friendly and formal. Partner to junior clerk. "Madame has gone to change her clothes. Perhaps wee Sally would like to do the same. There's a parcel there."

She flung her arms around her father's neck, dipped quick curtsies to Macdonald and Peter Maclaren, then darted from the room.

"A winsome wee lassie, Angus." Fergus Macdonald's eyes crinkled in his leathery face. "And a fine welcome home. It's no every day ye show 'em ye can beat the Athabascans either. Here's to ye and to your canoemen."

"I'll drink to them too." Cameron filled a glass for his son, then raised his own with the others.

"Now while ye're pouring me another dram, here's your five guineas." Macdonald stacked coins on the table. "And I'll buy the rum for the regale tonight. A half keg for each canoe. Ye can arrange that, Mr. Maclaren?"

"Indeed, sir." Peter Maclaren tugged a notebook from his pocket, looked up a page and made an entry. "Ten kegs. That will cost you. . ."

"Later, mon, later." Macdonald waved his hand airily, then he looked back sharply. "Ten *wee* kegs, mind. I'll be getting my brigade off at three in the morning. And I'll take forty bags of pemmican too. Ye can charge it to the. . ."

Duncan sipped at his drink. It was a bright room, this. Four good windows with real glass looked across the square to the main gate. Curtains of blue blanket were drawn back and neatly tied. There was a fireplace with a whitewashed chimney at each end — Quebec style, with high openings. Rushlight sconces hung on the walls. The furniture was home built and solid — desk, tables, chairs, wardrobe, bureau, bookshelves. Bright, woven rag rugs livened up the wide-planked floor. There were embroidered cushions on the chairs. A colourful finger-woven mat covered the table. It was comfortable, warm, a real home.

Maclaren broke in on Duncan's thoughts. "Mr. Cameron, you'll see to it, if you please — the rum and the pemmican. Mr. Seymour keeps the keys to the liquors. You'll find him in the clerks' quarters, no doubt." He spoke deliberately, with a rather pompous ring. He looked pompous too, with his heavy face and developing jowls.

Then he carefully wrote an order in his notebook and made a copy on another page. He took out his penknife, cut the original from the book and gave it to Duncan.

"No need to go right now." He was trying to sound affable. "When you've finished your visit. By the way, I drew straws to allocate rooms in the quarters to you new fellows."

"In the quarters?" He wouldn't be living here then? At home?

"You didn't fare too well, I'm afraid," Maclaren went on. "The end room's rather cold. But, well. . .no favouritism, y' know."

"No favouritism, Mr. Maclaren?" Duncan tried to speak lightly. "You mean no choice. We're out of school now. Couldn't we clerks sort that out ourselves?"

Maclaren eyed Duncan narrowly a moment but made no retort. Then he turned to Angus Cameron. "I hope you'll agree, Mr. Cameron. I gave the whole establishment the afternoon off — after the packs are in, of course."

"Indeed." Cameron nodded.

"Verra formal and tidy at Ile-à-la-Crosse, aren't ye noo?" Macdonald growled. Then he slapped his host on the shoulder. "He always was, this father o' yours, young Duncan Cameron. Careful. Aye, and canny. Ye can do worse than take a leaf oot o' his book." He picked up his glass and banged it firmly on the table and roared, "Except when it comes to pouring drink for his friends!"

At the other end of the room by the fireplace there was a table with two chessboards. Each had its ranks of pieces, beautifully carved. The boards were cleverly crafted of inlaid wood with different grains. Well-filled bookshelves lined the walls.

"Books. Aye. He's built a fine collection, eh, laddie?" Macdonald joined him. "Up here it's better to be addicted to books than to drink." He laughed and thumped Duncan on the shoulder, and pulled a volume from the shelf.

Duncan had kept his school-bred interest in books. It had been enhanced at the Letelliers, and he'd brought a husky pack of them up here with him. One of his handsome French editions was, in fact, warmly inscribed to him in Marianne Letellier's careful convent hand. Macdonald had spotted it when they were waiting out the wind at Michipicoten on the way up from Montreal, and he ragged him unmercifully.

"A liking for Molière, have ye, Duncan Cameron? They have a library in yon warehoose in Lachine, do they noo? And the bonniest librarian, I hear." He didn't miss a trick.

Macdonald raised his eyes from the page. "Duncan, when ye've read a book, remember, put it doon and pick up another. Ye can always read it again later. Meantime, there's more books i' the shelves and fish i' the sea, and girls i' the world."

He snapped the volume shut and put it back in the shelf. "Did ye look at the lassies on the way up here? They seem a wee bit different from the young ladies of Montreal, do they? Well, I'll tell ye, Duncan — there is a difference."

He paused and narrowed his eyes, then he lowered his voice confidentially. "They're here, laddie," he breathed. Then he threw back his head and shouted, "They're *here*!"

He was a roughshod old rogue, Fergus Macdonald. If only his own father would talk to him a bit like that, maybe they'd know each other better. Not that you expected to be friends with your father. But. . .well, their talk didn't seem to get any further than facts, events, instructions.

Fergus Macdonald glanced over at Cameron and Maclaren, still talking seriously, then back to Duncan. He seemed to read his mind.

"Ye're father's close-mouthed, Duncan. It's a good trait — not like me. He likely hasna told ye about his affliction?"

"Affliction, sir?"

"Well, ye should know. It's the stones he's got. The doctor at Fort William told him to have a care and take Turlington's Balsam and to see him next summer. It could mean the surgeon's knife, ye ken. But he's a tough one. Dinna fash! Here now, what's this?" He swung about.

"Och! Madame and bonnie Sally and all the wee bairns. A sight for sore auld eyes, I'll tell ye."

Duncan's mother stood in the doorway, smoothing the full pleated skirt of her new dress in quiet delight. It was of soft blue-grey wool with a high white collar, buttoned down the front. A wild rose bloom, beautifully fashioned in gleaming silver, hung from a fine chain around her neck.

Sally was beside her, holding the baby. Raymond, a five-year-old, and little Cat stood shyly on her other side. Each of them had on new clothes that had come a whole summer's travel from the finest shops in Montreal — including the baby's delicate lace cap.

The little ones eyed Duncan cautiously. His smile finally brought a shy response from Raymond and a happy laugh from Cat.

"Over here, the lot o' ye. Stand in front o' the hearth where we can see." Macdonald herded them over. "And the master o' the hoose too. Och! Angus, my friend, the sight of ye like that, and even a white-haired old reprobate like me will rush off to get married. They should a' be in a grand painting. D'ye no agree, Mr. Maclaren? The king and queen o' Ile-à-la-Crosse, and a' the royal family!"

Duncan's eyes were on his mother. She spoke to her husband in rather musical Cree, but it was too quick for him to understand. Then she changed to slow and careful English.

"Thank you, my husband, for all your gifts." She turned her eyes to Duncan and the lines in her face softened. "The best gift is my firstborn son."

She reached out and spoke his name. He went to her and she put her arms around him and

36

pulled his face to hers. He felt her tears mingling with his own.

It was a noisy, exuberant homecoming night. The Ile-à-la-Crosse guide and interpreters and those with special positions like Ti'moine Tremblay were quartered with their families inside the palisade. Ti'moine spoke three Indian languages and owned a large number of dogs, so he had special duties and privileges. Leo Bedard, by right of long service, had a room for himself and his latest wife and child.

Some of the rankless ones were already absorbed in the Indian encampment. They would disappear when the Indians did, to winter camps and traplines. A few newcomers slept under the canoes — as did the men of the Athabasca brigade — if anyone slept that night at all.

The hunters in the Indian encampment had killed some moose a couple of days before, and Peter Maclaren had bought enough for a feast for all hands. Fergus Macdonald's rum was shared, traded and consumed. It fuelled a great round of dancing and singing around blazing fires, and it brewed up some spirited fights. The Athabascans certainly weren't going to leave without revenge for losing the race. The closed gate and palisade were more use that night for keeping out carousing voyageurs than for keeping any enemies at bay.

Inside it was by no means quiet either. Dinner had been arranged by the Ile-à-la-Crosse clerks at two long tables in the Great Hall to honour their grand bourgeois and the visiting gentlemen from the Athabasca. It was a raucous affair and ill-controlled by Peter Maclaren.

Food and drink in plenty were served up by canoemen, who must have been well paid to entice them from revels of their own. Duncan saw Coco Pinet among them, neatly dressed, with greased-down hair. Trust Coco to find his way to a good thing! And he'd get a bit extra for playing his fiddle later on.

"You'll try some of our Madeira, Mr. Macdonald? It goes well with the moose nose."

"Och aye. You rascals live well, Mr. Maclaren. Now Mr. Balfour. . ." Macdonald called to his own senior clerk. "I certainly hope ye've brought some o' this fine wine to entertain your own bourgeois come winter!"

Balfour's unsmiling face grew even longer. "I greatly regret, sir, that due to economy measures, the gentlemen's mess at Fort Chipewyan will for the first time in history be. . .bone dry."

Cries of "No! Never! . . ."

"Aye, gentlemen. I must bring to your attention the minutes of the annual meeting of the partners of the North West Company at Fort William, 15th August, 1808. *Whereas*. . ." He rose to his feet, puffed his cheeks. Balfour could always be counted on for some entertainment.

"... *Whereas* strictest economy must be exercised to offset the advantage the Hudson's Bay Company has in shipping in and out of said Bay, and *whereas* it has become the custom among certain gentlemen to take up excessive space in company canoes for..." He ticked off his fingers. "...private trade goods, undeclared paquetons of furs for private trading, hams, salt beef, barrels of oysters, white sugar, coffee, kegs of Beluga caviar, casks of port and Madeira wine..."

"Oh, that'll no refer to us, Mr. Balfour." Fergus Macdonald threw up his hands in mock horror. "You young bucks perhaps, but Mr. Cameron and me, we're threadbare, half starved, frugal...teetotallers."

The laughter subsided. Balfour went solemnly on. "And *whereas* in certain canoes — for the sole comfort of said gentlemen — ladies have been carried..."

"Ladies! Never, never!" from Macdonald.

A howl of laughter filled the room. It was a legend in the northwest that Fergus Macdonald was one of those who never travelled without "his girl." He had gone on doing it in spite of the rules laid down every year. The girl had changed from time to time, but Macdonald's custom had not.

"If ye'd paid heed to the rule, Mr. Macdonald," Angus Cameron raised his voice above the noise, "your canoe would have been a good deal lighter today. Ye might have won the race!"

"Och no, Angus. Ye're dead wrong. Dead wrong. Why, she's just a mere wee slip of a thing."

Cameron shook his head helplessly. Duncan wondered what he was thinking. Probably that discipline up here was always a problem and the Fergus Macdonalds of the company didn't help. If you got right down to it, though, any Nor' wester alive would follow old Fergus to hell and back. The fact that along the way he'd be bedded down warm in his tent with a lass, while the rest slept half frozen on the bare ground, would not make one whit of difference! Some men were like that.

"And furthermore. . ." Balfour got back the crowd's attention. "Furthermore, gentlemen, you'll note the resolution of 1806 whereby the partners did resolve to cut expenses by permitting no new women and children to live with employees at the company's expense. . ."

"Quite right too. Quite right."

"Therefore, young bachelor gentlemen — Messrs. Farquhar and Benson and MacGillivray and Cameron and the rest — no Indian brides. No wives in the fashion of the country for the likes o' you. Unless. . ." He raised his hand. "Unless, of course, gentlemen, she's a bourgeois' daughter."

Laughter shook the room. Fists banged the tables. Balfour sat. The wine was passed again.

"Speaking of bourgeois' daughters," Benson

40

said across the table, "did you ever see such a comely lass as Rebecca Campbell down at Bas de la Rivière?"

Farquhar chimed in. "Not to look in the cradle there, Benson. She's barely thirteen." Benson was an older fellow — near thirty.

"Aye. But a year or two. . ."

"Get your bid in early then, before I do!"

None of them, thought Duncan, would have the poor judgement to mention Sally Cameron in the same way. She was very nearly of that age, though. It was something of a shock to think about it.

"There's Nancy Spence over at the Hudson's Bay fort, Mr. Benson, and some others." It was young Seymour, whose voice had barely cracked. He looked very earnest. "Would they count as bourgeois' daughters?"

"Spence? Did ye say Spence, laddie?" Fergus Macdonald looked across at Cameron. "Magnus Spence? At Cumberland House ten years back? Dull old dodderer."

"A decent man, though."

"Decent or no, he moves like molasses. Like the rest o' them." He looked down the table. "Gentlemen, young Master Seymour and a', mind this. It took the Hudson's Bay Company a full hundred years to find their way from York Factory to Cumberland House. That's because they move like molasses, and they won't move at a' till they're told by their masters in London.

41

But that's no the way o' the North West Company."

"If we amalgamate, sir," Benson ventured, "couldn't we ship out through Hudson's Bay and? . . ."

"Amalgamate? Amalgamate!" Macdonald exploded. "Let's hear no talk of amalgamate. The Hudson's Bay Company arrived on the shores o' the bay a hundred and forty years ago wi' a charter — from an English king, mind." He almost spat. "But they just sat on their duffs. We pedlars from Montreal didna sit. *We* were first up to Frog Portage — Frobisher and Primeau in '74. *We* were first right here at Ile-à-la-Crosse. Peter Pond was in the Athabasca in '78."

He swallowed his wine and his eyes flashed. "That's thirty years ago — when I was your age. And Alec Mackenzie went doon his river in '89, then west to the coast. And Davey Thompson's oot in the Columbia right noo. The North West Company is always first."

His heavy brows pulled down and he glowered around the whole company. "Gentlemen, we'll no stomach those poachers much longer. Run 'em oot, I say. Chase 'em doon the rivers to their blasted bay and let 'em swim for it. This country's ours, I tell ye. All of it. It's *ours*. Amalgamate? To hell! Right, Mr. Balfour?"

"Right, Mr. Macdonald!" Balfour banged his glass on the table. "But unless our friends at Ile-à-la-Crosse move quicker than they do in filling up our glasses, old Molasses Spence will take away all their trade, and we'll die o' drought before we get home."

"Och aye," Macdonald laughed. "And young Mr. Seymour, if Magnus Spence's daughter takes after him, she'll be decent, and dull, and built like a barrel, and slow enough for any o' you young bucks to catch."

A strong chord sounded from a violin, and in moments Coco Pinet's music had every man there pounding the table and roaring out the words of the old canoeing songs.

Drinking, singing, dancing to the fiddle, feats of strength and a roaring game of hunch-cuddy-hunch — Athabasca versus Ile-à-la-Crosse. In that game Wee Willie's bulk gave Athabasca the edge. Gavin Farquhar brought out his pipes and he played a wild pibroch. It would have gone on all night, but at a quarter to three o'clock Fergus Macdonald lurched to his feet. "Athabascans," he bellowed. "To your canoes, the lot o' ye. We're awa'."

He stood a moment, ramrod stiff. Then his eyes glazed. Overcome by the drink, he toppled slowly backwards and thundered to the floor like a felled tree. He lay there snoring. Balfour rallied the Athabasca clerks. With a cheer they picked Macdonald up, raised him shoulder high. Led by the piper they bore him out across the square and down to his canoe. Farquhar said later it was like bearing a Viking to Valhalla. But Fergus Macdonald, Duncan thought, would never die.

3
Nancy Spence

"We really would like to see a good deal more of you, Duncan — your mother and me. Sunday afternoons would be a good time for visiting her. You could stay for our Bible reading too." Angus Cameron looked up from his cup of tea. He seemed oddly uneasy. "But you do see, d'ye not, that I have to treat you like every other clerk?"

"Oh, I understand, sir." Duncan stirred more maple sugar into his cup, trying to keep the tightness from his voice. His father had already made that point clear by inviting him to breakfast second.

Benson first, then Cameron. Farquhar next week. The new arrivals in alphabetical order for the ritual private breakfast with the grand bourgeois. That was fair enough. But he hadn't been asked back to his own family's private house since the memorable day he'd first arrived.

"It's well known at the council, Duncan, that I'm dead against sons serving directly under their fathers. I've always made that clear when appointments have been discussed."

"With respect, sir, I know of a lot of cases. And in Montreal. . ."

Cameron raised his hand. "Others have their own way about it, Duncan, and Montreal is different. In fact, if your mother hadna made such a plea, you'd not be here now. You'd have had a visit and gone on to join Macdonald."

"I'm glad, sir, that one member of my family wanted to see me again," Duncan shot. He made himself look straight into his father's eyes. He could feel his anger rising. Maybe he'd have been better off with Macdonald.

Cameron frowned. He said carefully, "It's my intention that you should stop here for a year, then go to the Columbia district. Mr. Thompson's agreed to take ye. Your future's there. Whether ye believe it or no, Duncan, I have your best interests at heart."

Best interests? The best interests of a rising young clerk certainly were in getting his experience in the northwest. But as to his future, that lay back at the centre of things in Montreal.

Cameron finished his cup and put his hands flat on the table. He smiled stiffly. The creases between his eyes weren't nearly so deep, and he looked rested — better than he had on the trip up. Duncan had a sudden urge to reach out and touch one of those hands. He shifted in his chair instead.

He was a striking man, Angus Cameron, his

long Highland face and strong jaw with the cleft in his chin. That big hooked nose that gave him his Indian name, Crooked Nose, his eyes set deep and blue as the sky, his hair iron grey. He was respected. Purposeful, fair and even-handed. Steady as a rock, they said. Sober. Maybe a bit of a Bible thumper. That didn't go down well with some. The fur trade wasn't noted for its morals.

"My best interests, sir?"

"Aye." He leaned forward. "You've done very well, Duncan, in mathematics and science — everything at school. I'd like you to know I'm proud of you."

It was the first time anyone had said that.

"And your apprenticeship. Raymond Letellier tells me you did better than anybody we've had in the company for years. With the right experience, laddie, you can be a partner in Cameron and Letellier when I retire. Even a partner in the North West Company."

Duncan looked down at his father's hands still lying there. They were big, capable, blunt-fingered hands, freckled and nearly as white as the tablecloth. His own hands, brown and slim and only inches away, were an infinity apart.

"Dolts like Wee Willie MacGillivray become partners without even trying." Duncan looked up, tried to make it sound flippant. "But a half-breed has to be that much better, is that it, sir?"

Cameron's eyes darkened. He looked back at

his son for a long moment. "Aye," he said quietly, "it's true. And you and I both know that's the way life is, and you and I will never change it. But it won't stop you, Duncan Cameron. You have the ability. And you have the ambition. Maybe. . ." He dropped his eyes. "Maybe too much."

He leaned back and shifted awkwardly in his chair. He poured himself the last of the tea, mustering words.

Finally, "It's just, Duncan, that. . . Well, you're your own man, I know. But you can be your own worst enemy. Those reports. . . I have to tell you this. They speak highly on your ability, but too many of them say you've a wee chip on your shoulder and a sharp tongue wi' your seniors. Everyone needs friends, Duncan, and that's no the way they're made."

The last of the leaves were stripped. The pelicans flew south at their stately pace. So did the cormorants and the loons. Huge flights of geese and swans paused to feed on the flats and in the bays. Men, women and children all turned to killing, plucking, splitting, salting and storing hundreds of them for winter food. The nets produced a fine harvest of fish for smoking and drying. Out in the garden the women dug potatoes and turnips and onions. The fall hunt brought in moose and caribou. Smoke enveloped the drying racks and hung a blue haze in the still air. The sod-roofed glacière — still with enough of last winter's ice among the sawdust — filled with fresh meat.

All hands were occupied preparing for winter — except the clerks and their apprentices. Eternal ledger entries, inventories, victualling lists, work records, wage sheets, stock musters, sorting and stowing, equipment checks. On it went. Duncan and his fellows spent untold hours in the counting room and the storerooms and the trading room on endless stuffy chores. Each of them longed to be out there with the hunters and the other lesser folk, and out from under the schoolmasterish eye of Peter Maclaren.

Gavin Farquhar was philosophical. "In a few weeks they'll all be wanting in here where it's warm." Farquhar was a good sort, the same age as Duncan and the only bright spark in the bachelor clerks' quarters. As for the others, Maclaren seemed always on his dignity. He couldn't relax even at the mess table after a dram or two. Benson tended to drink morosely on his own, and young Seymour and the other juniors had their own protective clique.

"Six days shall ye labour, my friend." Farquhar poked his cheerful jug-eared face and unruly hair through Duncan's doorway on Saturday night. "As tomorrow is the Sabbath, will ye no join me in slaughtering some o' God's wee creatures wi' your fowling piece?"

48

They went out with their guns to a crisp dawn and walked for miles shooting grouse over partly frozen ground powdered with snow. They downed a dozen green-head ducks and pintails in the back pond as well, and at noon they were back with wet feet and their game bags full.

Coco Pinet, who had been hired by Maclaren as messman, was ready with buckets of hot water. Bathed and changed into his best suit, with freshly pressed shirt and stock and polished shoes, Duncan was down from his room in short order.

Farquhar let out a whistle. "A frog he would a'wooing go, eh, Master Cameron?" He raised a hot toddy to him. "Your green waistcoat and a' that. And what lassie would such a handsome fellow have his eyes upon, might I ask?"

"None. Like a dutiful fellow, I'm visiting my mother."

"Good for you. Like a scheming fellow, I'm a'calling on the bonnie Ma'm'selle Lisette Favreau."

"You and ten others!" Duncan grinned.

He took half a dozen birds as a present for his mother, and headed across the square to the Cameron house. He went around to the back door.

That first of the Sunday visits always dwelt in Duncan's mind. Stepping into the warm kitchen, lit only by the fire, with Rose Flower waiting for him, was like picking up some treasured childhood belonging misplaced for many years, conjuring memories from the deep and happy reaches of one's mind.

She sat crouched beside the fire. A blanket framed her face. The firelight softened her lines and she had a serenity that made her beautiful. Duncan sat beside her. Her face, the smell of smoke on the blanket, her gentle kiss, the quiet voice and those words of warmth and greeting. He was back again, a little boy, remembering — the teepee of his grandparents, Cut Hand and Snow Bird, those special sounds and smells, the murmuring voices, the unspoken words. . . . And the feeling of being loved.

He read a book with Sally and drew pictures of sailing ships and cities for Raymond. He rode the little fellow around on his back on all fours, and played cat's cradle with his younger sister. As far as Cat was concerned, the string game had been invented and named for her alone. She showed her big brother endless, quick-fingered variations. The four of them laughed and chattered. Baby Malcolm, fat-cheeked and beady-eyed, crawled about and crowed and watched them happily.

Rose Flower stayed by the fire, watching her children, but just outside their circle. As Duncan left, he looked down at the stark angles of her face, darkened by the white collar of her dress.

"Good-bye, Mother," he said. "I have enjoyed the afternoon."

She answered him in Cree and he leaned forward, trying to understand. She did not intend it, but it was a rebuke. They had scarcely spoken. For the whole afternoon he and the children had talked in English, and she had barely understood.

The great expanse of lake turned to a sheet of glittering glass. Then came heavy grey skies. Snow fell, the wind moaned around the eaves and snapped at the parchment windows, the nights drew in. The lake ice boomed. Water in the hand basins froze by morning. Snow, shovelled from the paths and doorways, piled up in banks. Winter was here.

Duncan gazed out the counting-room window — it was glass-paned for better light on the ledgers. Half a dozen children over there were having a great game tunnelling in the snowbank. One of the bundled figures looked like his brother Raymond.

"Mr. Cameron, this balance. . . Mr. Cameron!"

"Mmmmm?"

"Mr. Cameron!"

"Sir? Oh, yes, Mr. Maclaren. I'm sorry. . .just thinking."

"Thinking! So that's what it is you're doing. High time, perhaps." Peter Maclaren drew a breath and puffed out his cheeks. Here it comes, thought Duncan. Maclaren loved to use his authority in the counting room — especially with him. Equally, all the juniors enjoyed getting around their chief clerk when they could.

"Is there something wrong, Mr. Maclaren?" Duncan caught Gavin Farquhar's eye and stifled a smile.

"Wrong. Aye. Here you've been diddling and doodling with your pen and wasting good ink all over yon valuable paper, and there's no. . . Och. Will you look here." He plunked a sheaf of papers on Duncan's desk. "It's your Hudson's Bay account. I know full well Magnus Spence owes us more than that. He bought eighteen bags of pemmican, I remember it. I let him have it in September. Eighteen bags! They're on this invoice, look. But the statement. . ."

Duncan let him go on. He frowned. "Oh, that's very careless of me, Mr. Maclaren. Thank you for spotting it. Can I. . .well, I should make it right without delay. Why don't I take it over to Mr. Spence myself?"

"Aye. You should do that. No dragging your feet, though. You start the inventory tonight."

Duncan pulled on his capote and his red toque, winked at Farquhar, who signalled a silent thumbs up. Outside, young Raymond spotted him from the top of the snow fort. "Can't catch me, Duncan," he piped. "Can't catch me. . ."

Duncan sauntered closer. He made a sudden pounce and tossed his small brother laughing and squirming right over the bank. Then he bolted, screaming mock terror. A gaggle of small fry shouted after him, hurling lumps of snow. At the gate he sucked in a lungful of the cold clear air and turned towards the Hudson's Bay establishment.

The path was well beaten, mostly by children. They were always running back and forth, including Sally and Raymond. Officially, of course, the older people of the two companies only met on business. It was a good mile and the wind was blowing. Better than the counting room, though. Besides, he'd not been over there before and he'd been itching to find out if Magnus Spence's daughter was really built like a barrel.

That rascal Farquhar had a smug look about him these days. He kept dropping hints that he was getting on well with Lisette Favreau and that everybody else should steer clear. There weren't many other eligible girls around — they got snapped up so young. No harm then in exploring more distant fields — just so he could report back to the others, of course. Marianne Letellier was back there in Montreal, after all.

The wind was bitter cold. Forty years of growing population meant that every tree had long since been cut from this end of the peninsula. The baldness made for more breeze in summer to keep the flies down, and, of course, the open space improved defence. But in winter it was bleak and windswept as the open lake.

Inside, the post looked run-down. It was no more than half the size of the Nor'westers'. But simply being there made it a thorn in Angus Cameron's side.

Children's voices echoed around the yard. They were playing on the fur press beside the storehouse, seeing how far they could teeter out on its long projecting handle before they toppled into the snow. The steady *eee-aaaw eee-aaaw* of a whipsaw came from behind one of the buildings, and axes thunked in the wood yard.

It was nearly dark, and here and there a window glowed. At the head of the little square, light showed from the Chief Factor's house. Real glass. Duncan wondered how many letters to his London lordships it had taken Magnus Spence to get those few precious panes sent up from the Bay. That would be the counting house to the left of the Chief Factor's.

He opened the door without a knock and stepped into the warmth. Three faces turned towards him, white ovals in the semi-gloom.

"Still at it, gentlemen?" Desks stood against the wall. Above each a rushlight guttered. A solid glow came from the fireplace at the far end. That would be the chief clerk's spot — closest to the fire and furthest from the door.

"I've always heard you men from the Bay just work, work, work. Now I see it with my own eyes. It's past four o'clock." He turned to the older man, who was standing by the fire. "Mr. Clouston?"

"And who might you be?" The acid voice went with the long face and shiny domed forehead.

"My name's Cameron. North West Company. Clerk. Good day to you, sir." He swept an elaborate bow.

Clouston caught the mockery in Duncan's voice. He looked coldly at the lithe young intruder in his plain capote and moccasins and thick black hair. In spite of the wide mouth and cheekbones and his darkness, he had the Cameron stamp.

"Cameron, the younger, I presume — unless Master Crooked Nose has lost some years and changed the colour of his skin." An educated Orkneyman from his voice. "To what do I owe the doubtful pleasure of your visit?"

"I have an invoice here to discuss with Mr. Spence, which may be of doubtful pleasure to him. I just thought I might find him here."

"You can discuss it with me. What is it?"

"It's that matter of unpaid pemmican." Duncan held the folded invoice out between two fingers, his eyebrows raised. Clouston took a pace forward and reached for it. Duncan twitched it away from the sweeping hand and tucked it back in his pocket. "And as it's well known that you have very little in your larder, Mr. Clouston, I think it's a matter Mr. Spence would prefer to. . .ahh. . .negotiate himself."

It was a shot in the dark. He certainly had no mandate to negotiate anything, but it was worth knowing whether they were shy of food. Clouston's glower told him that they were.

"Of course, if he's not about. . ." Duncan pulled on his mitts, "you could give him my compliments and say it could be discussed whenever he chooses to come over. And, of course, there'll be no chance of any meat, meantime."

"You'll find him at home," Clouston snapped. "Here, Tompkin, show Mr. Cameron over to the Chief Factor's house and see he keeps. . ."

"Oh, don't trouble yourself, Mr. Tompkin."

The little fellow stood confused. He couldn't have been more than thirteen.

Duncan swept Clouston another bow, stepped out in the cold and pulled the door shut. That had given them something to think about. He swung around, grinning to himself, and barged straight into someone in the narrow path. He went down — or rather she did — and Duncan stooped to give a hand.

"Please excuse me, I didn't mean. . ." He took her arm and helped her up.

"It's all right." She stood and brushed the snow from her skirt. "You'll be Mr. Cameron?"

"Why, yes. . .Miss. . ." All he could see of her was a head of glossy dark hair.

"Well, my father, he saw you from the window. He said will you come and see him before you're awa'?" It was a musical voice, with a lilt and an accent nearly like Sally's mix of Cree and Scots.

She looked at him. Her eyes were big and set wide apart and the most lustrous brown he had ever seen. She was nearly as tall as Duncan and her gaze was disturbingly direct under thick black eyebrows. She was big, yes, and erect and graceful.

"Are you Miss. . .Miss Spence?"

"Aye. Nancy Spence." She bobbed a quick curtsy. "If you'll come now."

The door behind him flung open and there was young Tompkin shrugging on his capote. Clouston peered narrowly over his shoulder.

"Oh, it's quite all right," Duncan called, "Miss Spence will see I don't get into any mischief, I'm sure."

He turned and offered her his arm with a flourish, as though escorting her to the dance floor. She smiled, her teeth strong and white against the brownness of her face. Suddenly she gave a quick nod and put her hand on his arm. The counting-house door slammed shut behind them.

"Your Mr. Clouston seemed a little sour," he said. "Is he always that way?"

"Oh, I've never seen him laugh. Perhaps he's not got much to laugh about. I don't think he likes it here."

"Do you?"

She looked at him. "Why. . .of course." It was

almost as though she'd never considered the matter. Then she said, "But for me it's home. It's not for Mr. Clouston."

They were at the door. She lifted the latch and opened it to warmth and light.

"Welcome to the house," she said and smiled again.

4
Harry Whistler

"Aye. Mr. Cameron. Welcome to the house, indeed."

Magnus Spence was short and broad, with a heavy head topped with a knitted toque. If he had a neck at all, it was wrapped around and around with a woollen muffler. He wore a long coat of red duffle that stretched around his belly and came right down to his ankles. It seemed he had been doing some sort of handiwork, for its front was speckled a variety of colours and it was scattered with sawdust and chips of wood.

"Ye'll take a toddy wi' me? Aye? A glass o' toddy at the end o' the day. A good wee comfort it is." He drew Duncan to the fire. "Your coat. Here, Nancy, lass, Mr. Cameron's coat. And ye'll mix the toddy for us."

He stretched his stubby-fingered hands out to the fire. He wore gloves with the fingers cut out. His knuckle joints were swollen with arthritis.

"Aye. 'Tis the time o' the year again. The cold creeps right into these old bones come winter." He spoke as ponderously as he moved. "Sit ye doon then, sit ye doon."

Duncan took one of the chairs by the fireplace. Spence placed a log upright in the blaze, then creaked down into the other chair.

"Well then, I'm pleased to meet Angus Cameron's son. I could tell the minute ye set foot inside the gate. The way ye walk and stand like him, tall and straight. And your face. Aye, a strong likeness. And how is he, your father?"

"Oh, well, sir. Thank you."

"Did he send another move wi' ye then?"

"Move?"

"Och, aye. Ye didna know we've had a chess game going, oh, nigh a full year? Look ye here." Spence heaved himself up and led Duncan to a chessboard on a small table. A game was in progress, but there was only one chair. Spence picked up the white Queen and fondled it.

"I'm white, ye see. Your father's move that wee Sally brought over this morning was Rook to King's Bishop four. Now d'ye see what?. . . Ye do play the game, Mr. Cameron?"

"Oh, I do, sir, but I'd be no match for you." The chess piece in Spence's heavy, stub-fingered hand was beautifully carved. The board was too, with its inlaid squares of different-coloured woods.

"Ye noticed your father's board and his pieces are like these?" The old fellow's face beamed with pride. "A wee giftie it was, from Magnus Spence to a good friend."

He waved a hand modestly at the tidy little workbench under the window. A gleaming rack of chisels, knives and gouges hung above it. There was a half-finished carving of a goose in full flight. How could those grotesque old fingers do such delicately beautiful work, Duncan wondered. What a fine gift his father's chess set had been.

"Ye'll take him back my move?" Spence handed him a folded scrap of paper. "Aha, the toddy. Thankee, Nancy, lass."

Nancy was back with two steaming pewter mugs on a small tray, inlaid as elaborately as the chessboard. Along with the mugs came the rich smell of cinnamon, cloves and rum.

"Mr. Cameron first, my dear." Duncan saw the smile touch her lips and thought how nicely that generous mouth of hers turned up at the corners. Smiling carved a slender vertical crease in either cheek. It seemed to be for him then, and he returned it over the edge of his mug.

She really was a handsome girl, he thought. Not pretty. No. Her nose was big and straight, and she had high cheekbones and those heavy eyebrows nearly met in the middle. There was a slight curl in the dark hair that framed her face. Her strong jaw and straight white teeth seemed to go with the rest of her.

As for the rest of her, if she'd ever been the "barrel" described by Fergus Macdonald, she'd certainly outgrown it. She had a firm full figure and a slim waist and walked with the grace of the Cree side of her family — not her Orkney father's.

"Ah, my Janey." Magnus Spence's voice brought Duncan around.

A dark woman wearing a kerchief, shawl and the familiar black skirt and leggings had come quietly into the room. Her face was laced with wrinkles. She had deep-set eyes, and her hair was grey-streaked and pulled back tightly from her forehead. She looked pinched, dry as a stick and too old to have children as young as the peak-faced little girl who peered at Duncan from behind her mother's skirts.

"And bonnie Charlotte too. Come along then and meet Mr. Duncan Cameron. Sally's brother he is. Mr. Cameron, meet my good woman and wee Charlotte."

"Madame Spence." Duncan bowed. She inclined her head. Charlotte ventured cautiously out, and when Duncan dropped to his knee to say hello, she rewarded him with a smile and a self-conscious curtsy.

"Janey, will ye no join us a wee?" Spence's face was like an open book, Duncan thought. There was no questioning the pleasure he gained from his family — or his wood-carving. His eyes followed his wife as she sat on a folded blanket by the fire. Charlotte nestled at her side.

"She's my youngest, ye ken. The boys are all grown and flown, as they say. Working at Albany Post and York. Well placed too." He settled in his chair. "Now, Mr. Cameron, will ye no sup wi' me at our mess table before ye go? It's a long cold walk on an empty stomach."

"My thanks, Mr. Spence." Duncan declined. If they were to have had their meal here in the house, he'd see a bit more of Nancy perhaps. But women never joined the men at the mess table. "I'm expected back and I only came over to sort out the charges for the pemmican you bought in September."

" 'Twould be a time for ye to talk wi' a few men fra' the Bay. Get to know them, instead o' fighting." He sounded rather wistful. "Your father and me, live and let live is the way we see it. Fergus Macdonald, though, and his ilk. . . There's no a doubt about it, Mr. Cameron, some of your Nor'westers wi' their brawling and bullying and debauchery, and abusing the Indians, and flooding the country wi' liquor. . . Though not your father, mind. And it's no one-sided, I'll admit." He shook his head. "And we'll no change it. Och! About this pemmican."

"You see here, sir. . ." Duncan explained the entries. Spence furrowed his brow in concentration.

"Gi'e me the invoice and I'll initial it, and Mr. Clouston will pay ye on your way. There. Your Fergus Macdonald would never ha' let me have that food, but your father's policy is different." He nodded slowly. "All this trouble. In the Athabasca, up at Reindeer Lake, the Forks, on the Saskatchewan. . .everywhere. Servants will follow their masters, ye ken, and if the gentlemen fra' Montreal canna set doon wi' the gentlemen fra' the Bay, then. . ."

Magnus Spence continued doggedly on his theme. Why not form one company — stop all this destructive nonsense? The Indians were certainly not fools. They played one against the other. So up went the price of furs and pemmican and fresh meat. And up went the amount of rum they demanded before trading could even begin. And the more they drank, the greater their loss in self-respect and the less they trapped and hunted.

Duncan's eyes strayed to the figure of Nancy, busy at something in the dimness across the room. There was a lightness in the way she moved. She held herself so well, proudly even.

". . .and the fewer furs they bring in, the higher the price. No, Mr. Cameron, it's a vicious. . . Mr. Cameron?"

"Oh. . . Oh, indeed, sir."

Of course, it was all very well for Magnus Spence to talk. As a minor Chief Factor — a salaried employee — his influence on the Hudson's Bay Company's governors in far-off London was just about nil. Angus Cameron, though, and Fergus Macdonald and the other partners in the North West Company — they had everything to say about such matters. The trouble was they were such a proud, varied and fiercely independent lot that they found it hard to agree on anything.

"We do have the Royal Charter, and by rights

you Nor'westers are trespassing, but. . . Och! It'll no be easily solved." Spence shook his head dolefully. "Likely not in my time in the company. I'll retire in a couple of years, ye see."

"Oh. Where do you plan to settle then?" Duncan asked.

Magnus Spence pressed his lips together. There was a long silence, as though everyone in the room was holding his breath. Duncan stole a glimpse at Nancy. She was standing very still, not looking.

Spence shifted uncomfortably in his chair. The old man's forehead was pulled into a frown. Then he spoke softly, with his face to the fire as though he wanted no one else to hear. "Oh, that I'll have to decide closer to the time. But there's no place in the Indian country for an old dog who canna pull his weight anymore. . . . Ah, Nancy, lass."

She had come with the jug. "Ye'll have us tiddled, Nance." His cheerfulness seemed forced. "Mr. Cameron, ye'll have another wee touch, I'm sure."

Nancy's eyes weren't serene now. They were somewhere else, and they were shadowed, shut off.

"I. . .I. . .thank you, sir, but no. I must be away." Duncan got up from his chair and turned awkwardly to Spence's wife. She was holding young Charlotte close and her eyes were on the fire. Duncan said a formal good evening, but she didn't raise her head.

"Ye must visit again then," Spence said heartily. "Ye're a chip off your father's block, and I've a real liking for him." He heaved himself up. "Nancy, will ye show Mr. Cameron back to Mr. Clouston?"

He steered Duncan over to the door with a hand on his shoulder while Nancy got their coats. He dropped his voice. "Ye mind, Mr. Cameron, I'd have no objection if you was to call on my Nancy. She's an age, ye ken, and a son o' Angus Cameron. . ." He patted Duncan's shoulder and gave him a ponderous wink.

Nancy came with the coats, and they walked across the darkened square in silence. They went slowly, neither wanting to break off. But they didn't speak. At the snowbank near the counting-house door, Duncan stopped.

"Look here, I'm sorry. I must have said something back there that upset you, Nanc. . . Miss Spence."

"You can call me Nancy if you like." She looked straight at him. "It's just that none of us likes to think about Father going away and not coming back. It will happen someday. It does to most everyone. But. . ."

"I'm. . .I'm sure he'll make the best arrangements for you all. I mean. . ." He looked down and nudged the snowbank with his toe. "Look. . . Well, I. . .I have some skates. We've cleared a place on the ice. Would you like to come? On Sunday?"

He hoped she hadn't heard her father's invita-

66

tion to call on her. It would be years till he thought of marrying anyone at all — and it wouldn't be up here anyway.

He would like to see her again, though. Her face turned to his, and even in the darkness he could see her smile and nod. His mitt off, he put up his hand and touched her cheek.

There was a sudden shout from the direction of the gate. It was followed by the distant *hike-hike-hike* of a dog-runner urging on his team. Soon they caught the crunch of a toboggan on the snow. Now they could see its ponderous bulk coming through the gate.

Behind them the counting-house door opened. Light flooded the snow. "And who's this? What?. . ." Clouston's thin voice. "Cameron! What the devil are you doing. . . Oh, Miss Spence, I didn't see you. . ."

"Hoa. . .hoa." The heavy-loaded toboggan came to a halt only a few feet away. The runner stepped off its tail and stamped his anchor into the hard-packed snow. It was barely needed. The dogs had had enough. The lead dog sat panting breathlessly, tongue lolling, ears laid back, looking around for its master. The others flopped, panting, some rolling to bite at the snow, all of them exhausted. Another shout from the gate. A second toboggan came in and pulled up behind the first.

"Come on, my man, get me out of this damned thing." An imperious voice came from the depths of the carriole.

The dog-runner helped his passenger out of the cocoon of caribou skins. A tall man stepped clear, stretching and flexing the stiffness out of his joints and trying to stamp some warmth into his feet.

"Benighted bloody country, this. Four days banged about in that ice-cold coffin. Half frozen all the way from Carlton House." It was hard to make out the man's face but he sounded English. "And how long am I going to stand here, god-damn it, before someone invites me in?"

"Oh, ah, indeed." Clouston finally spoke. "And who might you be, my friend?"

"Your friend I'm not, and never will be unless you get me inside bloody soon." He was definitely English. He had the same way of speaking as the young garrison officers who idled about Montreal. And even in the dark he had their air of self-assured superiority.

"Name's Whistler. Harry Whistler. From the governor's office in London. I've business with Magnus Spence. You're him?" He stepped closer to Clouston.

"I'm Clouston. Chief clerk. If you'd like to come with me to the officers' quarters. . ." Clouston spoke carefully. He was impressed with Whistler but he tried not to show it.

"No. You can take me straight to the Chief Factor. Dare say he'll have some food and drink." He half turned to the dog-runner. "See that my baggage gets to the Chief Factor's house."

He swung around, stepped out and nearly ran

68

into Nancy. "Who's this?" he snapped. Then, "I say, I'm so sorry, Miss. . ."

Clouston said, "Miss Nancy Spence, the Chief Factor's daughter — Mr. Whistler."

"Charmed, Miss Spence. We'll see more of each other, I'm sure." There was that English air of owning the world. "And this fellow here?"

"My name's Cameron," Duncan said evenly. "North West Company." He put out his hand.

"Cameron!" He ignored the hand. "Clouston, don't tell me these bloody pedlars are allowed to run around loose in here. They'll steal you blind, my good man. What the hell's going on?"

He took a pace towards Duncan. "That's not Angus Cameron. Too young. Oh." He paused. His face was suddenly lit from the door opening. Under the fur hat it was clean-cut and handsome. His eyebrows were raised and there was a contemptuous twist to his mouth. "Oh, of course, this will be one of his brown bastards."

Duncan measured his words. "I don't know you, Mr. Whistler, but you're being offensive."

"Offensive!" He jerked out a rather high laugh. "I'll show you offensive, my lad. Clouston, just pitch him out the gate, will you, and then take me to Mr. Spence. I've damned well had enough of this."

"Don't you do it, Mr. Clouston." It was Nancy Spence. "And I'm not so sure my father will want to see someone who behaves like Mr. Whistler."

"He probably won't, young lady, but he'll

learn. Get on with it, Clouston. And by the way, Cameron, don't come back. *There's* a good fellow."

"Here, you two." Clouston gestured to the two dog-runners. In a flash each had Duncan by an arm and they spun him about. Wiry men with knives at their belts. No point fighting.

Over his shoulder he saw Nancy lunge forward, then jerk to a sudden stop. Someone — Whistler — had caught her arm.

"So much for your insolence, Cameron." Clouston was enjoying getting back at him.

He heard a gasp of outrage from Nancy and a light laugh from Whistler. "Now, Miss Spence, perhaps you'd show me the way?"

"You can find it, sir, yourself."

The two impassive men silently frog-marched Duncan across the square and out the gate. Suddenly they slammed him facedown in the snow. A moccasined toe caught him hard in the stomach. He picked himself up, retching, and heard the gate swing shut.

Whistler. Now who the devil?. . . Someone to be reckoned with, certainly. And whatever his business at Ile-à-la-Crosse, it looked as though things would be a good deal different from now on.

The stars were icy pinpricks in the sky and the wind moaned around the corner of the darkened palisade. Duncan shivered with the sudden cold, pulled his hood up and trudged the lonely windswept mile towards home.

5
Wolverine

Things *were* a good deal different. Duncan reported the bare facts of the evening's events to Peter Maclaren, then formally to his father. Neither of them had heard of Harry Whistler.

Angus Cameron was puzzled. "If he's just making trouble on his own, that's one thing. If he's come here to stir up Magnus Spence and put some ginger into his people, that could be quite another."

"Mr. Spence was very friendly, sir," Duncan said. "And Clouston wasn't expecting Whistler at all." He didn't mention Nancy. He hadn't to Farquhar or the others either.

"We'll keep our eyes peeled. Stand by for trouble, Mr. Maclaren, and pass the word to all the posts. I want to hear of anything you can glean about this Harry Whistler."

Duncan was too distracted to worry about it, or anything else for that matter. The icicles at the counting-room window flashing like jewels in the slanting sun, the shouts of the children running by, the antics of the whiskeyjacks, the raucous conference of ravens on the roof across the yard — anything and everything took his mind from his work. And it would drift to Nancy Spence and the Sunday coming up.

Sally came to see him in the counting room at the end of the next day when everyone else was gone. She had brought a book to read, and her copy-book as usual, so the two of them could spend an hour on her lessons. But there was an intense look on her ever-cheerful face. She was bursting with news, disturbing news.

"They wouldn't let me inside the Bay fort today, Duncan."

"Who wouldn't, Sally?"

"Oh, the man at the gate. A guard. They've never had one before."

"What did he say?"

"Just that only Hudson's Bay people were allowed, and to shove off. But I wanted to see Charlotte and I had Father's chess move for Mr. Spence. So I just went around to the trading-room gate. You can squeeze through. . .well, if you know where."

"And if you're a weasel like Sally Cameron," he laughed. There was something of the little animal about her bright-eyed alertness and the way she would watch, then move in sudden darts. "You went to the Chief Factor's house?"

"Yes, I did. But there was a man there who was really rude. He said he'd take a stick to me if he saw me again, or anyone else from over here. He spoke rathah like this. . ." She gave an imitation of an English accent. "Charlotte called him Mr. Whistler, I think."

"Oho. Make sure you tell Father about that." He paused, trying to sound casual. "Did you see Nancy Spence, by any chance?"

Sally raised her eyebrows and looked at him sideways. "Nancy? Ohoho! So Duncan Cameron's sweet on Nancy Spence!"

"Nothing like that, Sally, but. . ."

"I know, I know. Charlotte told me. Oh, yes. Nancy said she can't come skating on Sunday. She really wants to, I think, but it's that Mr. Whistler — because she made sure he didn't hear."

Sally spent most of their lesson time teasing him. Half his mind was over in the Hudson's Bay Company's establishment. The other half was busy hatching out schemes. If Nancy was being kept in there against her will. . .

Duncan looked in on Ti'moine Tremblay. The little fellow threw his door open with a broad smile. Behind him three tiny Tremblays scuttled up the ladder to the sleeping loft. By the time Duncan was settled at the fire with a cup of tea, they were peering down at him huge-eyed, like a trio of curious chipmunks.

"You told me, Ti'moine, that you'd teach me to run dogs this winter. Can we start?"

"Indeed, m'sieu." He wrinkled his forehead

quizzically, then grinned. "Usually the gentle-men, they ride in the carriole. But certainly. . ."

As well as paddling and running dog teams in winter for the company, Ti'moine bred first-class animals. Looking after forty or more dogs was no small task, and his Cree woman and their big brood of children were always at it. They hunted, hauled their fishnets year round, and kept their own storehouse for equipment, fish and meat. Between children and dogs, there were some who said that Ti'moine ran one breeding operation to support the other, but had forgotten which came first!

"I'll show you everything I can, but the best is to come out with me en derouine — to visit all the families on their traplines, and trade with them." He flashed a smile. "Then you can be the dog-runner, m'sieu. That's how to learn. And Ti'moine will ride in the carriole like the fine gentleman!"

With all his cheerful bounce Ti'moine was steady and thorough. Like everyone else, he turned his dogs loose in summer on an island well offshore. But unlike most others, he made sure his were properly fed. He selected pairs for breeding very carefully — but not for conformity. They were a mixed lot in appearance. He bred for strength and stamina and spirit. Sometimes he staked out a specially chosen bitch for mating with a wolf. Wild ancestry marked his best lead dog, an alert unsmiling bitch he called Belle Dame. He certainly had a fine kennel for his

74

pains, and he showed it off to Duncan with pride.

The lively pups that his boys were training to run in harness behind their mothers were kept in a separate pen. "They must understand the stick, m'sieu. But the carrot is best." A chorus of yowls and barking greeted them, and Ti'moine dispensed tidbits to much tail wagging. "Like children, eh? And the elders teach the younger ones their manners. See old Gran' Bleu there?"

He had bought that fine white Eskimo dog with the strong red markings years back to add strength and endurance to his line. The old patriarch with his broad chest and slit eyes still pulled with great strength and endless endurance. All the pups he had sired had inherited the best of him. He ruled the pack. None of the younger dogs was prepared yet to challenge his domination.

"Their day will come, m'sieu, but for now if I put Gran' Bleu at wheel dog and Belle Dame there at lead, for a long haul I beat any team in the whole nort'wes'. You'll see in spring."

When the March gathering took place, Ti'moine always made a tidy sum betting on his own racing teams. Also, of course, he was paid for the use of his dogs when on company business — running the winter express or taking one of the traders on a circuit. All that, plus the proceeds of selling his first-rate pups and his canoeman's wages with the singer's bonus, and Ti'moine Tremblay was a man of means.

He took his other responsibilities seriously too. His wife was well bedecked with silver jewellery. She was able to buy plenty of the best woollen cloth for clothing, she had pots and pans and implements. The family was always properly fed and looked after. So were his old parents away back on the St. Lawrence, whom he hadn't seen for years.

"We'll have to wait for a long run, m'sieu, until after the New Year. Tomorrow I take le gran' bourgeois to Green Lake and up the Waterhen. He goes every year before Christmas. This evening, though, you can help me harness up some young dogs. Also my oldest boy, Simon, will take you out while I'm away."

And before Christmas the news began to trickle in. It wasn't just the Nor'westers who were going out and bringing in the furs. Someone else was out en derouine. No longer, it seemed, were the English from the Bay afraid of their own long winter shadows.

Duncan was outside when Jo, the Iroquois, brought Maclaren back in from Buffalo Narrows with a light load and a long face. Someone had been there before him. The second pair of toboggans with Favreau and Leo Bedard was equally light. The next day it was Angus Cameron, who only growled and strode off, leaving Ti'moine to tell the story.

"At Canoe Lake, m'sieu, it was very bad." He

76

shook his head as Duncan checked the few furs they'd brought. "Moose Runner, he always has a good catch in early winter. We always hold back the rum. This time his camp is a mess. No skins. No furs. Moose Runner and his wives and his brother — all of them in the teepees stinking sick with rum. We find one boy, m'sieu — I know him — frozen dead. Just by the teepee. Ten paces. . ."

He shook his head. "The fire wood is all burned. The dogs, they rove about, eating everything they find. The small children are afraid of them and they have run into the bush to snare rabbits. Me and le gran' bourgeois, we bring them back and feed them."

"Good God! Who'd been there, Ti'moine? Did they say?"

"The children say a trader who they didn't know. One of the English. With dogs and a guide. He took all the furs and all their meat for nothing except a great deal of rum. They left no powder. No shot or ice chisels, or axe heads. Nothing that they will need. Only these."

He pulled an empty rum jug from his carriole. It was clearly marked "HBCoy."

Rum. The English. Not old Magnus Spence himself. He could scarcely get around, even with dogs. And he was dead against trafficking in rum. Clouston certainly wasn't the type to fill Indians with it. He was much too careful to ever set a foot wrong. The rest? According to Maclaren, no one from over there had been out like that for the last three years, and none had any experience. They just stuck inside their own four walls and hoped for trade to come to them.

So, Whistler must be behind it. Harry Whistler. The new broom.

Ti'moine Tremblay looked at Duncan, his round little face screwed up and his eyes narrowed. "Like a wolverine, m'sieu. Whoever it was. Stealing what is ours, and what he leaves behind he fouls."

Wolverine. Yes. For Mr. Harry Whistler, perhaps the name was right.

6
The New Year

It was Hogmanay. The celebration of the New Year. To Duncan it could be the beginning of a new life. Tonight he had the feeling that this was where he belonged.

He watched the dancing from the end of the Great Hall. It was a gigantic cavern, alive with figures leaping and spinning to the wild music of fiddle and pipes. The blaze of the fires roaring at either end lit up the dancers and threw fantastic shadows upwards through the beams. They danced and swayed up there like some weird company of their own.

Everyone was in from the traplines and winter camps, and from the small posts. There had been some trading, but mainly it was a family gathering. Haultain, a raucous likable fellow, had brought his bride in from La Loche. There was Pringle over there, the Post Master at the Waterhen. He was half Ojibway and married to one of the Favreaus. They had a new baby to show to the proud grandparents. Pringle and his father-in-law seemed to get on famously. They had been drinking the baby's health since Christmas.

And Christmas had been the turning point for Duncan. On its eve, Sally and Raymond burst into the bachelors' quarters. Neither of them had taken time to even pull on a capote.

"You're to come to dinner, Duncan. To the house. Mother says."

Raymond puffed, "Right now. And to stay the night too. Will you play horse?"

For the first time he was greeted by his father as part of the family, not just as a junior clerk. For the first time since he was six years old he slept under the same roof as his mother and brothers and sisters. For the first time that he could remember he sat at the decorated table with them all. He listened to his father say grace, watched him carve the roasted goose.

He heard him calling his mother by a name, not just referring to her second-hand as "Madame." "My Bonnie," he called her, and he made a proper name of it.

He stood and raised his glass. "My children, Duncan, Sally, Raymond, Catherine. Please stand and drink a health with me." He turned aside to the baby watching bright-eyed from his cradle-board. "And I know, wee Malcolm, that you'd join us if you could. Here's to my Bonnie, to your mother. The great lady in our lives. And may every one of us live always in love and happiness together." He repeated his words in Cree.

"Together," Rose Flower replied. It was as though she had said "Amen." She turned her deep dark eyes to each in turn.

His father then praised Duncan's progress. In his reserved way, of course. He said he was pleased to see him earn regard amongst his fellows through the standard of his own good work. But Duncan knew that was not why he had at last been welcomed here. It was his mother, Rose Flower, who had turned the tide. He felt her warmth embrace them all.

And finally today, the first day of the year, when Peter Maclaren had knocked on the door to invite le grand bourgeois and all his family to the feu de joie, he — Duncan Cameron — had been with them.

He was proud to stand beneath the flagpole wearing the lustrous coat and hat of carefully matched-up lynx his mother had made him. He glanced down at his finely beaded moccasins, caught Sally's eye and warmed to the pleasure in her face. She had spent untold hours making them for her brother. The many-coloured sash around his waist had been woven by wee Cat's patient fingers. Raymond had drawn a picture on birch bark for him and had put it in a wooden frame. The stickish figures were clearly the Cameron family. They stood smiling on the shore, with the house behind and Duncan alone in a canoe.

His mother stood, serene beside her husband, in her pure-white winter weasel coat. Royal ermine. The tiny black dashes of their tails fringed its edge and cuffs. Baby Malcolm's cradle-board was in her arms. Its wide protecting hoop of silver glinted in the sun.

The sun, in fact, was barely over the top of the palisade. The day was bitter cold and breath plumed white from the festive people gathered in the square. A cheer went up when the bugle sounded and the bright new flag broke out against the hard blue of the winter sky. Then stumpy old Favreau snapped his orders. The fifty musket men stationed at even intervals all around the square presented arms, then in quick succession pulled their triggers.

The spurts of flame, the blast of each, rippled down one side of the square, across the end, then up the other. Each shot added to the mounting thunder, echoed from the log walls, stunned the ears. Right on the heels of the feu de joie came the bellow of the cannon in the north bastion, then the south, then east, then west.

For a long moment there was silence. The muskets pointed, rock steady to the sky. Smoke hung, motionless as morning mist. Then a long sigh escaped the crowd, then a shout, a cheer. The ranks broke and the morning filled with laughter. Small boys grabbed their father's empty muskets to run off playing hunter. Gavin Farquhar's pipes groaned into life. Groups clapped to the music and danced on the snow, keeping warm.

The New Year always started with the ceremonial handshake with le grand bourgeois, and
the decorous kissing of his wife. Duncan watched
his mother pass the baby into Sally's arms, then
offer her cheek to Peter Maclaren. Seniority
placed him at the head of the line. Then Benson,
then young Duncan Cameron. She had a special
smile for her own son. The Post Masters followed.
Haultain, Pringle. . .

Led by Favreau, the engagés filed by. In line
they jigged against the cold. They chattered like
magpies, strutted their new hats, mitts, sashes,
moccasins and coats to each other, shouted with
laughter at their own and other's jokes.

"After your kiss, la femme du bourgeois will
have eyes for no one else, you say, Coco Pinet?"
Spoken so Duncan could hear.

And from Leo Bedard, "Heh, M'sieu Cameron.
Such a fine coat. I have une belle brunette for
you. For that coat she is yours. And I t'row in
one of Ti'moine's running dogs!"

But the handshakes with le grand bourgeois,
the salutations to Madame, were courtly and
respectful. His mother commanded it as much as
did his father. She had dignity about her, and
strength. The slight inclining of her head as she
turned her cheek, the smile for each in turn.
And she knew them all by name.

So the day had gone. A tot of rum for everyone to drink the health of a brave New Year.
And special rations, a marvellous pudding made
with raisins and dates and peel, buffalo suet and

a bag of precious flour.

It was a festive, even raucous crowd around the gentlemen's mess table that evening before the ball. All of them were in their best. Duncan wore Cat's sash outside his coat and he had shined his shoes to mirror brightness. During the string of toasts, Angus Cameron rose. He was splendid in his kilt and sporran, jacket with silver buttons and finely ruffled shirt.

"Gentlemen." He looked around the table. "I must remind you. As always, I have invited Magnus Spence and the officers from over there and their families for the ball."

He'd said 'their families.' Nancy would be coming! Duncan knew he'd have to be quick off the mark to keep ahead of those other eager clerks.

". . .the new man Whistler's stirring the pot, there's little doubt o' that. I know what Fergus Macdonald had to say. He's a good friend o' mine, but I want to make this clear: My policy is peace. In my district we'll beat the Bay people by being quicker and cannier and giving our Indians fair play. It's good furs we want at a good price, and not drunken Indians and broken heads. Aye." He looked around the table. "And if anyone needs a reason, it's simply better economy."

Now everyone was in the Great Hall. Post Masters, clerks, apprentices, interpreters, artisans, canoemen, their Métis and Indian wives, and all the children who were old enough to dance a step or two — or young enough to still be at their mothers' breasts. All of them were there, and all in their finery. Against the wall too, at the other end flanking the fireplace, were half a dozen Cree hunters. They crouched there watching impassively, scarcely acknowledging as their women were swept off to dance or returned to them after.

The music of the gigue went on and on. Coco Pinet sat on a chair on a table-top, his fiddle bow flying, moccasin pounding. Beside him Gavin Farquhar's fingers worked furiously on the chanter of his pipes. Gradually they built the rhythm up and up and up until the dancers' feet could barely cope. Then suddenly they stopped. Pinet stood up and flourished his bow to the breathless cheers.

"A bumper for the players!" Someone handed each of them a well-filled mug. They'd been playing for an hour non-stop.

Women went back to their places against the walls. The gentlemen gathered at their punch bowl. Others clustered in laughing, sweating groups to swap jokes and swig from each other's flasks. The children formed groups to clap out their own music and chase each other about. Raymond and Cat were among them, chattering in a cheerful mix of English, French and Cree.

Duncan watched Sally coming towards him, her hand on Peter Maclaren's arm. Her face was shining and her toes kept darting from under the skirt of her new dress. She was still dancing to the last gigue.

"This young lady's danced my legs off, Mr. Cameron!" Maclaren mopped his face with his handkerchief. Even he was having a good time.

"Isn't Coco Pinet the best fiddler you've ever heard, Duncan?" Sally's eyes were dancing like her slippered feet.

Then the outside door swung open with a bang and a blast of cold air. Magnus Spence, bulked in a heavy buffalo coat, filled the doorway. He stepped inside and stood uncertainly as the noise in the hall died. Behind and a head taller was Harry Whistler.

Whistler fitted the picture that had grown in Duncan's mind. Tall, fair-haired, handsome. The commanding look of one who expects lesser folk to do his bidding — and knuckle their foreheads too. A fine fur coat and high, polished boots. He looked coolly around the silent faces. He doffed the coat. Without looking at anyone in particular, he held it out. It was Coco Pinet who took it. Whistler wore a particularly elegant suit of clothes. Under his mitts, white gloves.

Next came Jane Spence, looking somewhat drawn, with young Charlotte. Then Nancy. She was wearing a red capote. With quick gestures she pushed back the hood and unbuttoned it. Her face was glowing from the cold. Her hair gleamed like dark copper. She stood still and straight, searching the crowd with her eyes.

"Welcome to the house!" Angus Cameron's voice cut the silence. Hand extended, he strode across the floor. Erect, dignified, impressive in his kilt, he towered above the squat and homely Magnus Spence as he shook his hand.

"A welcome, Mr. Spence, and to your lady and your family and all your people." He spoke loudly so all would hear. "Come inside and have something to warm you. . .and some music. Mr. Farquhar!. . ."

Nancy's eyes found Duncan. Her full lips curved into a smile that was like the summer sun, and it shone for him alone. For one moment there was no one else in the crowded hall. Their eyes held.

Then someone stepped in his way. He pushed quickly through the crowd. "Mr. Spence, good evening to you, sir. . .Madame." He bowed, turned, and he was facing Nancy.

"Miss Spence, if you please, this dance?" She nodded very slightly without speaking, relief showing in her eyes. Pinet's fiddle sang out an opening flourish, calling dancers for a reel. For a moment Duncan could only stand and look.

Her dress — unlike those wide black skirts and loose blouses with crossed-over shawls that most of the Métis women wore — was a bright yellow print, buttoned and fitting closely to her figure. Beneath it, cloth leggings and beaded moccasins tied with ribbons at the ankle. She wore a yellow ribbon in her hair. Duncan offered her his arm.

"No, old man, this dance is mine." The languid voice was right in Duncan's ear. It was Harry Whistler.

He was well built and a shade taller than Duncan. He had a flush on his cheeks, and there was a twist to his lips that spoke disdain.

"You are our guest, sir, and a welcome to you. But I did speak first." Duncan kept his voice level.

The man's eyes were ice-blue. He turned to Nancy. "Mine, Miss Spence." It was said with his self-possessed smile. But it was not a request. It was a command.

Nancy's lips tightened. She looked evenly at Whistler and put her hand on Duncan's arm. "Mr. Cameron did ask me first, sir. The next dance, perhaps."

Whistler's eyes narrowed, his flush deepened and his nostrils pinched white. Duncan rocked on his toes, ready.

Suddenly the music leaped to life. There was a whoop and a pounding of feet. Nancy tugged Duncan's arm. In a moment they were in among the dancers. They found a place in an eight and almost before Duncan knew it they were whirling and turning to the reel.

"What was that about?" They snatched odd words as they met, linked arms and swung before parting again.

"He seems to own the post. . . ." Her face was tense, her eyes troubled. Duncan watched her in the middle of the circle, one hand on her hip, the other curved above her head, her toe darting to the music. She held herself erect and her head was high. She moved with fluid grace. Her eyes, though — there was trouble in her eyes.

Then the dance was over. The gentlemen were gathering for a glass at the table by the door to Cameron's quarters. Duncan felt Nancy's hand in his. Whistler eyed them over his drink. She dropped his hand and headed for the women and children near the fire.

"Young Mr. Cameron!" Magnus Spence was a little flushed. He wore an ancient shiny suit of heavy black serge, which had been let out for him more than once, and a spotless white shirt and stock.

"Och, and it is guid to see ye." He stretched out his hand. He still wore the fingerless gloves.

"Ye've no met Mr. Whistler. Mr. Harry Whistler, who's to take charge at Ile-à-la-Crosse."

"We've had the pleasure, sir." Duncan inclined his head warily. Whistler turned half away.

"To take charge of what at Ile-à-la-Crosse, Mr. Spence?" Angus Cameron broke in good-humouredly.

Spence's heavy old face clouded. "Och, aye, o' course. Why, only o' the Hudson's Bay establishment, I assure ye. I'd hardly suggest he could take charge o' the likes o' you Nor'westers."

"Though the time will come." Whistler's voice was clipped.

"Taking charge of Nor'westers is hard enough even for Nor'westers, Mr. Whistler," Cameron said lightly, then turned back. "When will you leave then, Spence?"

"Come spring, I expect. Here, I've things to

tell ye." He pulled Cameron away by the sleeve.

Gavin Farquhar nudged Duncan's arm. "Here, have a dram." He laughed, then dropped his voice. "That Nancy Spence. She's not bad by half. Surely the old boy is going to marry her off, now he's leaving. Wonder why he hasn't before? She must be nearly sixteen."

Duncan shrugged.

"Oho! Are you first in line?" Farquhar grinned.

"At seventeen? Hah! Don't *you* get ideas there!"

"Dog in the manger. Lucky for you, I'm number one with Ma'm'selle Favreau. But look out, Benson's on the prowl."

He was a good fellow, Gavin Farquhar. Light-hearted. And you could depend on him.

"Well, back I go to the pipes! It's thirsty work, I tell you. Here's health." He tossed back his glass.

The dance went on. A strathspey next, and much slower. Whistler took Nancy to the floor. Angus Cameron offered his arm to Jane Spence, and Magnus took the cue to seek out Madame Cameron. Duncan danced with starry-eyed Sally and watched Nancy with Whistler. She danced without smiling, in the way of the Indian women, with a solemn shuffling step.

He said to Sally, "Do you still have a way of getting in and out over there, Weasel?"

"At Mr. Spence's fort? Oh, yes. And I know why you ask." She looked up at him with her impish grin, and teased him for the rest of the dance.

90

The evening rolled on. Drink flowed, noise increased and the dancing got wilder. Spence talked earnestly to Cameron by the fire. Children were spirited off to bed. The Bay people were cheerful enough, except for Whistler. Even the acid-tongued Clouston and frightened little Tompkin warmed up. A Bay fellow called Isbister began to lurch clumsily from too much drink. Whistler danced with Nancy or stood aloofly drinking, looking more disdainful and more flushed.

Clouston shouted over the noise, "Whistler's the favourite nephew of one of the London governors, you know. Bit of a rake back there, I gather. He got booted out of his regiment, so they sent him to the colonies. Lets us all know he's got influence — in that accent of his. He's as good as in charge already, and he'll not be good to work for. As far as he's concerned, us Orkney-men are all dolts."

"A frightfully perceptive fellow, what?" Farquhar chipped in with a credible imitation of Whistler. He raised his glass before Clouston took offence. They were all pretty good-humoured. Except for Harry Whistler.

A few of the men had teetered off, under the weather, but most of them were tireless. So long as the music lasted, they'd keep on dancing. Farquhar had had enough of his pipes and danced with Lisette Favreau. Coco Pinet fiddled on. His cap was on the edge of the table and now and then someone would drop in a trade token to keep him going. Leo Bedard joined in with his bones. Favreau step-danced to roars of applause. A scuffle started in a corner, and the snarling pair was pitched through the door to fight it out in the snow. Someone called for a song. Ti'moine Tremblay jumped up on the table to take the lead. Voices roared in response.

The lamps burned out. Only the fires lit the room. The gentlemen were draining the punch tub. Duncan found Nancy in a shadowed corner. Her eyes seemed luminous and huge.

"Will you take me somewhere, please?" Her voice was choked.

Duncan nodded and led her straight to the door that opened into his family's quarters. The fires in there had burned low and only one lamp was alight. She stood with her back against the closed door, her hands flat against it. The muffled sound of singing came through.

She drew a breath. "I'm sorry, Mr. Cameron."

"Duncan, please. If I'm to call you Nancy."

"Duncan, I'm sorry to bring you here. Mr. Whistler. He keeps. . .at me."

"What right does he have? Won't your father deal with him?"

Her shoulders sagged. "Father's so careful with him. Because of who he is. Whistler thinks he has a right to. . .everything."

"Even you?" He said it softly, his eyes on the fire.

She drew a deep breath. Then: "Yes." A pause.

"And Father's going away, you know."

"I heard him say he's retiring," Duncan said carefully. He bit his lower lip, put logs on the fire. "But where will he go?"

"Oh." She moved beside him and looked into the growing flames. "To his Orkney home. He's dreamed of it for years, I think. That's where he was born. It's natural he wants to go."

"Will he not take you? The family?" Duncan already knew the answer.

She shook her head. "The company won't allow it."

Spence would have precious little to retire on, Duncan thought. Even if he could afford to take his family without company help, what then? Nancy on a windswept Orkney isle? Marrying a fisherman or farmer. And part Indian. . . It had been tough enough for a half-breed boy in Montreal.

"You wouldn't like it there," he said gently. "They say there are no trees, or real lakes or rivers, or. . . Well, he'll make arrangements here for your mother and all of you." He groped for words. "Good arrangements, I'm sure."

"He's not saved much, but he's done his best." She moved over to Angus Cameron's chessboard, picked up one of the pawns, enclosed it in her hand. "It's all arranged with. . ." She swallowed as though she were choking. "It's all arranged with. . .Mr. Whistler."

"You can't mean it!"

She nodded, turned and looked directly at him. "Yes, I'm to be Whistler's wife. He'll look after us all."

"No," Duncan breathed. "You can't. He can't. Why..."

"I must. Father says we'll be far better off here. You just said that yourself. He says Whistler will be very rich one day. He can look after us well. He says it will be best for all of us. . . ." Her voice trailed away.

The fire popped gently. She turned her eyes to his. "You see," her voice sank almost to a whisper, "Mother's getting older. I'm all he has to bargain with."

"To bargain with. . . No!"

Whistler. And one day *he* would leave — when he'd had enough of the Indian country and the fur trade and of Nancy and the children they'd have. And Nancy would be passed on to someone else.

She shook her head and her jaw was firmly set. "No. I don't ever want to be Whistler's wife. But that's not the main thing."

She held the chess pawn to her lips and he could barely hear her speak. "The main thing is. . .we really want to be with Father. Wherever he goes. And he doesn't understand. You see, he doesn't understand how much we love him."

All Duncan could do was put his arms around her and kiss her cheek where the tears ran down, and wonder when the Camerons would face such sorrows of their own.

7
Sunday Morning

Sally took a note from Duncan to Nancy by her secret route and next day she brought the reply to him in the trading room. He was checking stock there alone after the New Year's trading.

"Well done, Weasel," he laughed, slipping it into his pocket. The nickname certainly fitted. Agility and courage got her into places where others couldn't or wouldn't go.

"Go on. Read it," she said. "I won't look."

"Sit over there, then," he growled. He picked her up and plunked her on a chest of tea. She certainly wouldn't leave until she'd found out all about it.

There was no address, but it was sealed with wax. Inside, Nancy had written in careful block letters: *Yes. Thank you. Sunday 9 o'clock. Back Bay*.

"Well, that makes you happy, Duncan, doesn't it?" Sally teased. Then her face turned serious and she dropped her voice to a whisper. "You're going to run away together, aren't you?"

"Sally, what the devil are you talking about?"

"So she doesn't have to marry that man Whistler. I know." She slipped from the chest and came over to him. Her voice dropped even further. "Charlotte said. And I hope you do. I like Nancy."

"Run away?" Duncan sat down and faced her. "It's nothing like that. We're just going for a Sunday picnic with Ti'moine's dogs."

"Will you take me then? Please?"

"Look, I'll take you out tomorrow with Raymond and Cat. On Sunday it's only Nancy and me. You'll keep it secret? Please?"

"I always keep secrets." She headed for the door, then turned back. "Oh, yes, Father wants two bottles of Turlington's Balsam. I don't think he's feeling very well."

On Sunday Duncan was up before the sun. Beyond the deep shadows of the palisade he saw it rise in a long low splash of red. Overhead the sky was clear, and out across the lake you could see forever. In the night the trees had gathered a frosty coating of ghostly white. The rising sun painted them fiery red and washed the surface of the lake pale pink.

Duncan found Ti'moine at his enclosure with two of his boys. Their breath hung white in the still air. They were laying out harness, and the dogs yapped, yowled and stretched and wagged their tails, sensing a run, eager to be on the move.

"B'jour, m'sieu. Fait beau." Ti'moine and two miniature Tremblays grinned happily. It was a glorious morning, though Duncan's hands ached with the iron cold when he took off his mitts to work.

"Ti'moine, this is your best harness." It was laid out on the snow ahead of the toboggan, ready for the dogs.

"Of course, m'sieu. You have on your best moccasins and your fine fur coat and hat. And the lady is very beautiful, one hears."

"Did Sally tell you that, Ti'moine?" Duncan tried to keep from smiling.

Ti'moine's eyes rolled to the heavens. So much for Sally always keeping secrets. "A bird, m'sieu. But I see he spoke the truth, eh?" His droll little face screwed up in a grin. "But, no, this is not my very best harness. I also have the set with the beaded saddles and the plumes for the dogs' heads. But that's only for weddings, eh?" He winked. "Whenever you're ready for that, m'sieu, Ti'moine will be glad to take you on your honeymoon."

Belle yipped happily, wagged her tail and nuzzled Duncan's hand as he untied her. He smiled and spoke to her and slipped the harness over her head, tucked her legs through and settled it around her shoulders and chest. She would lead. He ruffled her ears and went for another dog.

"Take Gran' Bleu too," called Ti'moine. "And Fripon with the flop ears for wheel dog, and

Ti'bleu and the three young ones there. Seven dogs. You'll go fast. To Montreal for dinner, eh? In the carriole there, I put an axe and extra skins and a kettle, in case you forget. And a few fish for the dogs, if you have to stay out overnight." He winked. "The weather, she can change, m'sieu. Or you may find some caribou. The lady. . . Who knows what can happen along the trail, eh?" He rolled his eyes.

"You're a rascal, Ti'moine, but thanks." What chance was there of keeping anything a secret?

This was no hunting trip, so Ti'moine had lent him his elegant toboggan, the one with the red-painted upturn in front and the carved back-board and the brightly decorated sides to the carriole. Duncan tossed in his snowshoes, gun and pack. He had tea, sugar, sultanas and raisins left from the great New Year's pudding, and a tender cut of caribou. He had a bagful of dried meat to chew too — good to keep you going along the way — but this was a day for a picnic.

He was off with a whoop. The dogs broke away in a sprint, tails high. He gave them a good fast run down the lake. Turning to circle back, the young ones stepped outside their traces, tangled and brought the whole team up in a snarling mess. Duncan waded in to sort things out. Gran' Bleu snapped at the culprits to make sure they knew who was in charge. Gradually they settled down from their morning excitement to a fast, even trot.

Belle kept looking back over her shoulder, not

quite sure of Duncan's voice. She questioned him when he wanted her to turn off the beaten trail into Back Bay and he had to lead her by the collar into the soft snow and wade ahead of her. They stopped in the lee of the willows.

The frosted branches were like spun sugar icing on a wedding cake. A grey jay examined the toboggan brazenly for food. A mouse skittered over the snow and disappeared. Feathery wisps of cloud began to climb the western sky. It must be very close to nine o'clock. He put his hand in his pocket to make sure the little present he had for her was there.

Gran' Bleu growled and peered around, slit-eyed. The dogs stirred and pricked their ears. Then Duncan heard the clack of a snowshoe and in a moment Nancy was there where the trail came down through the alders. She wore her red capote and had a carrying bag slung across her shoulder. She spotted him and stopped, looked quickly behind, then walked towards him with a light and easy stride.

"I'm so glad you came, Nancy." It was hard to find words. Her wide-set eyes. That direct open look. It denied pleasantries. Somehow with her you had to say just what you thought — no more, no less.

"Father thinks I'm out with Mother on her snare line," she said.

"What does your mother think?" He smiled.

"Mother thinks. . .I'm being foolish, but she'll say nothing." She took a breath. "And Whistler went off somewhere three days ago." Her eyes clouded. She bent down quickly and patted Belle. The dog whined happily and licked her face.

"Has he?. . ." Duncan didn't know what to say.

"Let's not worry about it." She shook her head sharply, pushed back her hood and turned her face towards the sun. It struck a sheen of darkened copper from her hair. She drew in a deep breath of the clear sharp air and looked off at the distance.

"Isn't it beautiful?" He could barely hear her. "Clean and beautiful." Then she looked at him. "Duncan, a girl is supposed to do what her father says about marrying. If only Whistler didn't hate us all. No, it isn't really hate." She tried a Cree word.

"You mean he looks down on you?" he asked.

She nodded, then suddenly she smiled at him and she was fresh and vital as the morning. "This is a day for us. Let's not worry."

She put her snowshoes into the carriole, then paused a moment. "I have a gift for you," she said. From her carrying bag she took a pair of gloves and held them out.

"Beautiful," Duncan breathed. "Thank you, Nancy, they're beautiful."

Perfect bleached-white deerskin, sewn so that not a stitch showed. There was moosehide on the palm for longer wear. They had gauntlets fringed with lynx to match his coat, and their backs were worked with a delicately twined design of flowers and leaves in multi-coloured silks.

His hands slid into the down-soft squirrel lining. "Perfect. A perfect fit. And perfectly made," he said. "But my poor gift for you is nothing."

It was a mundane piece of trade silver — a turtle, two inches long, with a ring to hang it by. There was no silver chain left in the store, so he had strung it on a loop of rawhide — plain babiche. When he gave it to her, though, she turned it over carefully in her hand, and her eyes shone.

"Will you please put your name on it," she said almost shyly. "For me?"

He took it from her and with his knife point he inscribed it carefully on the back. 'N.S. — D.C. Jan. 1809.' When he hung it around her neck, words stuck in his throat.

The snow was hard and smooth on the open lake, packed by the winds that had howled down from the north a few days back. Belle followed the blown-over trail without a pause and they headed northwest up the limitless expanse of Aubichon Arm.

Duncan rode the tail of the toboggan. He looked ahead over Nancy's hood and the backs of the briskly trotting dogs. Their tails were curled high, their ears pricked up. He could hear their even, steady panting. Occasionally one of them would snatch a bite of snow to slake its thirst. Belle's head was always on the move —

eyeing the trail, looking out ahead, glancing back to check the other dogs, to catch a glimpse of Duncan, listening for his voice.

He ran now and then, warming up, his footfalls squeaking high-pitched and hollow on the hard-packed snow. The dogs were moving well and he had to stretch his legs to keep up. He pulled his hood forward. Even this slight wind nipped the nose and chin.

He looked down at Nancy in the carriole, wrapped in skins. She must have sensed his gaze, for she tilted her head back. Her lips were parted. There was laughter in her eyes.

"You look so funny up there, Mr. Cameron, upside down."

He suddenly bent forward and kissed her. "That would be better right side up. Move ahead, Miss Spence."

He swung one leg up and over the backboard, followed with the other. The toboggan moved steadily along. He squeezed down into the back of the carriole, slipped a leg on either side of her, reached forward under the skins and hugged her back against his chest. He slipped his new gloves off and found the warmness of her hands, and their fingers intertwined.

"Hike hike hike," he called to the dogs. "On, Belle! Get on, Gran' Bleu, Fripon!"

She called to them too, and she laughed and laughed and so did he. Their laughter joined and it soared up, up, up to the giant sky — for the sheer joy of living on this lovely day in this lovely land and being with each other.

The dogs surged ahead. The toboggan whispered smoothly on. The sun climbed, striking diamonds from the snow. Her cheek against his own was firm and smooth and warm. Her eyelashes were long and black and they trapped tiny particles of ice. The dogs ran on and on. The toboggan flexed gently under them, gliding over the solid sculpted waves of snow. They turned and they kissed and held each other close. And there was no one in this whole wide lovely world except themselves.

How long did their magic carpet fly along the lake? The wisps of cloud above had thickened and the sun had paled a bit. Ahead, low down, the sky was clogged with grey. The air was a little softer, not so cold. Perhaps that redness in the morning sky had warned of snow.

"Hike hike!" The lagging pace picked up. How far had they come? It was hard to tell. That wide steep-sided opening to the left, though, must be Watchusk Bay. From his memory of the map, a stream ran in. A good spot to stop and boil some tea?

"Chaw, Belle, chaw." She pointed just that way. There was something dark ahead showing through the snow just off the shore. A rock near the stream's mouth?

Nancy stirred and turned her face to his. "I was. . .oh, dreaming, perhaps. I feel. . . Duncan, I feel so happy. Being with you. Whatever's back there, it doesn't matter."

He said, "We could just run on forever."

Her lips moved to his.

Then, "Why not?" he breathed.

Why not? Her eyes were deep brown pools.

"Why not!" Here, if you were capable enough to look after another as well as yourself, you did — and should. This was not Montreal. Here the social rules of whites did not apply. Why should they, in any case, apply to him? Or her?

They could live off this great land, as their ancestors had. And they could do it together. It was where he belonged in spite of all those years away. Here, with her. They belonged together.

The dogs yelped and the toboggan lurched and leaped. He looked ahead, over their backs, past pricked-up ears. They were stretched out, at a full run, going for something. That rock far ahead?

"Hoa, Belle! Hoa, you dogs. Hoa." They wouldn't slow. It wasn't a rock. Some animal, perhaps, killed by wolves or a hunter on the ice? The remains of a caribou or a moose? A raven circled.

Duncan was back on the tail of the bounding toboggan, dragging his foot, trying to slow the dogs. His snow anchor hung over the handlebar, its line running to the head of the toboggan. He tried to jam it into the snow but it bounced and wouldn't hold. If the dogs got into fresh meat, there'd be trouble. Fights, and the devil of a time getting them away from it and back on the trail.

"Hold on, Nancy, I'm going to tip it!"

She was up and out of the carriole as he rolled it, and the two of them hung on, bouncing and dragging over the snow and laughing until they brought the rig to a halt. The dogs still strained ahead, yapping and snarling.

Whip in hand, Duncan grabbed Belle by her collar and pulled her around. He fetched her two good clouts on the flank with the butt of the whip. She hung her head, ashamed. Then he and Nancy heaved the other dogs around behind her, straightened the toboggan and anchored it. Gran' Bleu snarled smugly at the rest and they settled down to watch, panting, tongues lolling from their run.

It wasn't a rock. It wasn't a dismembered caribou or moose. It was a toboggan turned over on its side. The bottom was towards them, the contents strewn about. The dogs were gone. So was the owner, whoever that might have been. The raven, perched on it, croaked balefully and hunched its wings.

The wind was up and he could hear it sighing in the jackpines on the slope nearby. Dogs barked faintly somewhere. His own team stirred and yipped and whined. A wisp of loose snow blew from under the overturned toboggan and whirled away.

The snow here was churned and stamped. Footprints and snowshoe tracks led to shore where the stream flowed into a small black patch of open water. The tracks disappeared through a fringe of alder and into the spruce behind.

But this toboggan now. He could see its tracks coming from the northwest. It had been heading down the arm towards Ile-à-la-Crosse. The winter express, perhaps, from the Athabasca? It was due about now. A sudden flapping and the raven flew a few yards and eyed them from the snow.

It was the express, all right. The skin side of the carriole was painted with a tidy rendering of the North West Company's tree and beaver badge and their motto "Perseverance."

And there was something on the other side they hadn't seen. Some sort of bundle in the snow, half covered by the carriole. Duncan heaved on the backboard handles. The toboggan rolled upright. He heard Nancy draw her breath and moan.

Lying on his back, grotesquely twisted, was a man. Moccasins, leggings, blue capote, blood-drenched. A dog whip in one hand, fur hat half buried in the snow. And the snow was brilliant red, and the head and face. . .the head and face were nothing. . .nothing but a bloody, mangled pulp.

8
Death on the Ice

"Who is it?" Nancy's voice was low and choked, and she was breathing hard.

Duncan felt his stomach heave, on the verge of vomit. He took her by the shoulder and turned her away. "It's our courier. It must be."

He looked along the toboggan's track. Endless frozen lake — narrowing, disappearing into nothing. The clouds to the west were now a glowering grey.

The track was fresh. So were the tracks that led to shore. They must be the killers'. And this was murder. Cold-blooded, pointblank murder. He felt the hair crawl on the back of his neck. His mouth went dry. Somewhere up in those trees. . .

"Nancy, I'll have to go after them. You heard the dogs. They may not be far." He headed for his toboggan.

"I'll come with you."

"You'll not. I'll just take my gun. If they're having to break trail up there, I can catch them on my snowshoes." He turned, his face set. "You stay with the dogs. If anyone comes but me, head for home. Please. And get word to my father."

"You'll need help."

"Look, Nancy, I won't have. . ."

Gran' Blue growled. The dogs stirred, hackles up, looking towards the shore. Three men came from the shadow of the spruce.

The leader was on the lake now, near the open water. He was awkward but fast on his snowshoes. He held a gun. So did the others. They fanned out on either side. There was menace in their stride.

He stopped ten feet away. The gun swung easily in his hand. He looked at them with narrowed eyes, glanced down at the body in the snow.

"A pretty sight, by God!" It was Harry Whistler. His face was stony and his eyes were cold blue chips. "A pretty sight indeed." Was he talking about the two of them, or about the dead man on the snow?

He said, "And I'd like to know, Miss Spence, just why you're here."

"That's my business, Whistler," Duncan said.

Whistler whirled and his eyes blazed. Then his jaw clamped and he said quite evenly, "I'll deal with that later, but you're lucky you didn't come an hour or so ago. You might have been ambushed too, you know."

"Ambushed?" Duncan looked at the two other men. The Orkneyman he'd seen at the ball.

Isbister, was that it? The other was an Indian he didn't know. A Chipewyan — flat face, broad nose. They both seemed ready with their guns.

"We just came into the head of the bay, over from Kazan Lake," Whistler drawled. "Heard shots, you know. We got here and those Indians — four of them — were picking over this poor fellow's body."

"Four Indians? Where are they?"

"They headed up there." He jerked his thumb towards the trail he had just come down. "We chased them for a couple of miles. They took his dogs, and they must have taken your letter packet too."

"Letter packet?"

Whistler gestured at the toboggan. "It's your express, so there must have been letters. I suppose those Indians were waiting for him."

Duncan's eyes narrowed. No Indian would try to rob an express. Couriers always travelled light and moved fast. They carried only their own gear and the fur returns and letter packs. What interest did Indians have in sheaves of paper?

"Whistler," Duncan said carefully. He had to watch this man, and there was Nancy to think about too. "I'm asking you to help me track down the people who did this."

"Track them down? I've already tried."

"A couple of miles," Duncan threw at him. "That's just a start. Come on, we'll go together."

"It's your bloody express, Cameron. Your business."

109

"A man's been murdered," Duncan gritted. "I'd say that's everyone's business."

"Just one of your damned northern Indians. No affair of mine."

"How do you?. . ." Duncan stopped. His spine crawled.

Whistler had done it. He'd killed the man — or one of his people had. He'd just tipped his hand. Nancy would catch that too. He hoped to God she didn't throw it in Whistler's face. If that man thought for one instant that she knew. . .

Whistler took a pace forward. "I'll tell you what *is* my affair, though. Miss Spence being here with you. You can take your own company's rubbish in, and that body. That's up to you. I'll take Miss Spence."

"Thank you, no, Mr. Whistler," Nancy said flatly.

"Indeed, I will." His voice was ice-cold. "Cameron doesn't need your help. You know your father's forbidden you to see any of the pedlars — or their brats. Come along."

He moved towards her. His men were close behind. He was smiling, and his teeth showed.

"No." Duncan moved in front of Nancy. "She's said no once, and that's enough."

Whistler's eyes narrowed. He seemed to coil, then he moved his gun. Duncan did the only thing he could. He swung his fist hard, caught the man flush in the nose. He heard it crunch. Whistler gasped, tripped on his snowshoes and went down.

"Nancy. The toboggan," Duncan shouted.
"Go!"

He whirled and jumped straight for the Indian,
got his hands on his musket. There was a flash
and a roar. He wrenched it clear. Again, the
Indian's snowshoes brought him down and
Duncan flattened him with the butt of his own
gun.

He took it by the barrel then and went straight
for Isbister, standing irresolute.

"Shoot him!" Whistler screeched.

"Stop!" It was Nancy.

Isbister froze, turned his head. Whistler was
on his knees, his nose trickling blood, staring up
at Nancy Spence. She had Duncan's musket to
her shoulder, aimed straight at Whistler's head.

"I'll shoot unless you let him go." Her voice
was tight and even.

"Gently, Miss." Whistler was suddenly very
cool. "Isbister, if she fires, you shoot Cameron.
Understand?"

"Aye, sir." Isbister's musket barrel swung to
Duncan's chest.

"Now, Miss Spence, which would you sooner
— the two of us alive, or Cameron dead? You
could miss me from over there, you know. But
you shoot, or move — he dies. Drop your gun
before I count five, or Isbister kills him."

He started to count. "One. . .two. . .three. . ."

Nancy looked at Duncan. If she fired. . . He
shook his head, trying to signal her. Even if she
hit Whistler, the other two would kill him. Then

God knows what they'd do to her.

"Four. . ."

"Nancy, it isn't primed." Duncan croaked it out.

"Not. . ." Her shoulders slumped. She looked at the musket in disbelief, then slowly let it drop. She turned to Whistler with utter loathing in her eyes.

"Next time, Whistler. . ."

Isbister's musket swung. Duncan should have seen it coming, should have ducked. The butt caught his shoulder, crashed up beneath his jaw. He felt himself flying backwards, saw shooting lights. He seemed to be in the snow. A monstrous numbing thump then, beneath his ribs. Another. Another. Then a crack on his head. Again it came. . .again.

Whistler's voice was a thousand miles away. "Leave him. The wolves will finish him. Cut his dogs loose. The wolves will finish him off. . ."

He was cold, very cold. There was snow against his face. A warm patch somewhere. Like a blanket. But he couldn't seem to pull it over him. He was lying in the snow, and it was dark. . .and cold.

Dog. He smelled dog. Something stirred and he heard a growl. He tried to raise his head and felt that it would split. Snow was falling. He could feel it on his face. There was a dog close beside him. He could feel the warmth. Belle? He spoke to her. She grumbled slightly, pushed against him and went back to sleep.

He came around again to the uncertain light of early dawn, with Belle's cold nose nuzzling at his ear. A surly layer of cloud hung low above the lake. How long had he been here? He struggled to his knees. His head. Oh God, it hurt. His shoulder too, and ribs. Pain shot through his jaw. He could just make out the smudgy outline of the shore through the falling snow.

He could see his toboggan. And the robbed express. It came back with a rush. Nancy. The murdered courier. Whistler. All of it. His stomach churned. He shivered uncontrollably, retched and brought up bile.

Nancy. Would Whistler harm her? He tried to pull his thoughts together as he lay there quaking. No. Likely not. She was going to be his wife after all. His wife. . .

He half crawled to his own toboggan. The dogs had stripped it of anything they could eat. But at least they'd come back here after they'd been cut loose. Four of them, anyway. There were four snow-covered humps apart from Belle who sat and watched as he sorted bits of slashed harness, tied cut ends together. He used the straps from his pack to make repairs. Somehow he got the dogs hitched.

It was agony. Everything about him hurt. Except his right foot. It was numb. Frozen. He could only stump about. He doubted if he could run at all. He mustn't let those dogs get out of his control. He'd be left behind. He longed to simply crawl into the carriole and sleep.

But he must get up that trail. The one that Whistler had come down. Soon the snow would blot out all the signs. His good foot hit something in the snow. His musket. At least he had that. He sat on the toboggan and loaded.

Painfully he led Belle to the start of the trail where it entered the trees. She gave a lively bark and wagged her tail. The others were tugging, whining, ready to go. He flopped on the toboggan and away they shot, moving quickly, with only Duncan's weight to pull.

The spruce thinned out. They climbed through jack pine, then took a swing to the right around a rocky face. A clearing, a steep drop down to the surface of the lake. Without the falling snow, this place would have a clear view, up and down the miles-long arm. And here the tracks stopped.

According to a blazed tree, the trail continued. There must be a lake at the top. But no toboggan or snowshoe tracks went beyond this very point. The dogs nosed about the clearing, sniffed and whined. There were no mysterious Indians. The only ones up here had been Whistler and his crew.

They had spent one night at least. The earlier snow was well tramped down. There were the poles they had cut to make a lean-to. He scuffed the freshly fallen snow. They'd brought up spruce boughs to sleep on, and for the dogs. Over there they'd had their fire.

And there were no other tracks. No one else had been anywhere near. There had been no stray Indians. Only Whistler and his men. They'd come up here to wait and watch. It was they who had ambushed the courier, taken the letter packets and fur returns.

Snow was swirling now. The world had lost its focus. Suddenly he felt hopelessly weak. His frozen foot gave under him. He flopped into the carriole, called out to Belle.

"Down the trail, Belle. Go for home. Hike hike hike. . ." He wondered if she would understand.

"You did as well as any man could." Angus Cameron stood with his back to the fire in the clerks' quarters. Duncan spooned in his third bowl of steaming rub-a-boo. His face was puffed. So was one ear. They'd been frozen a bit. The skin would peel, but the flesh would mend. His foot was bad, though.

He had a monstrous bruise all up his jaw from Isbister's gun butt. It was pretty hard to eat. They'd certainly given him one hell of a beating. But he'd not be alive at all if Belle hadn't led right through the snowstorm on her own.

"Is there any other evidence that Whistler did it?" Peter Maclaren asked the question for the third time. His pencil hovered over his notebook.

"Just that he and his people were there and no one else was. He lied about that. And how could anyone tell that a headless man is an

115

Indian — and a northern Indian at that — unless he'd seen him in one piece before he blew his head off?"

Duncan had had about enough of the inquisition. "And, in God's name, why would four Indians who didn't exist go after a bundle of fur returns unless someone in the Hudson's Bay Company put them up to it? And if someone did, then it's a hundred to one it was that bastard Whistler, anyway. And in case you didn't know it, old Spence has lost his grip over there and Whistler's in charge."

"That information came from Miss Spence, I daresay," Maclaren said drily.

Maclaren would bring that up — just to grind in the fact that he'd broken the rules. Duncan took sips of tea that someone had laced with rum. His foot was hurting like the devil. Thawing out. He hoped he didn't lose any toes.

"Yes, and it's reliable information." He knew his voice was shaking. "What the devil if I was with her?"

"Steady, Mr. Cameron." His father spoke. "I'm a sworn Justice of the Peace and I have power of arrest. If I'm satisfied there's a reasonable case, I'll take the three of them into custody. And I'll summon Nancy Spence to give evidence too. And perhaps her father. It's no small matter to take a party o' prisoners and witnesses clear to Montreal for a trial, but I'm prepared to do it. I've appointed Mr. Maclaren as recorder, and I'd be obliged if you'd give him all the information you can. . ."

Duncan pushed himself up from the table. "If you'll excuse me, gentlemen," he muttered, "I've some explaining to do to Ti'moine Tremblay. I've lost two of his dogs. If it wasn't for the others, bless their hearts, I'd be frozen stiff out there and you'd never have known one damned thing about all this. I. . ."

The faces around him blurred. The floor tilted. The table came up at him. He crumpled in a heap and the chief clerk and grand bourgeois carried him to bed.

9
Traitor

Duncan was mending in his cot when Gavin Farquhar told him how they'd tried to arrest Harry Whistler.

"Your father had the warrant in his hand but we didn't get any further than the gate. They slammed it in our faces. Then it was Magnus Spence up in the bastion arguing back and forth, with Angus Cameron down below, about the Canada Jurisdiction Act and who had the right to do what, and all that."

"And Whistler?"

"Oh, he was there all right, in the bastion behind Spence. Putting the words in the old duffer's mouth — just like a Punch and Judy show. Spence wouldn't give him up. Finally your father said they were sealed off. Anyone going in or out would be shot, and they'd get no food or supplies from outside until Whistler was delivered on a plate."

"How'd they like that?"

"You could hear Whistler laugh. Then he shouted down that any Nor'wester in range of their rampart gun would be shot without warning. And we had three minutes to clear out." Farquhar wrinkled his forehead. "He pointed the thing straight at us. I tell you, the hair stood up on the back of my neck when we were walking away."

Duncan shook his head. "Maybe we should have attacked them at night, taken them by force."

"That's not Angus Cameron's way. You know that. He goes by the law. He says they're low on food. They're depending on Moose Runner and some others to bring in meat. So we just ring them round day and night and starve them out. Oh, by the way, Tremblay went up for the courier's body. Not much left."

If Fergus Macdonald had been in charge at Ile-à-la-Crosse, Harry Whistler would likely be in irons by now and Spence's fort would be in flames. There'd be more blood on the snow. Maybe that was the only way. But then there was Nancy, other women too, and children. Stuck in the middle. And if there was fighting and the men got out of control. . .the worst things could happen to the women.

"Welcome back to duty, Mr. Cameron," Maclaren said.

Duncan's face was blotchy from the peeled

skin and he still limped, but he'd had quite enough of inactivity.

"You'll rotate with Benson and Farquhar here. Twenty-four hours duty. You have twelve men each and arrange your own patrols." Maclaren had a sketch map of the surroundings. There was their own fort near the point of the peninsula. The Bay's was closer to the mainland with a good half mile of open space beyond it before you got to the scrub with all the second growth. That's where the summer trail went through.

"The bourgeois sent word out that he'll cut off trade with anyone who brings meat to the English. So they'll have to get out to hunt for themselves, and on dark nights they'll likely try. The main thing is to stop any meat getting in."

"And maybe stop Whistler and his crew from slipping out?" Duncan asked. "If they get away, what's the point?"

"Yes, quite." Maclaren frowned. He hadn't thought of that.

"What do we do if we catch someone, Mr. Maclaren? Shoot 'em?" Benson was always direct. "You never told us."

Maclaren looked at his notebook. Eyes still down, he said, "Of course."

Of course. Just like that. Duncan wondered if Maclaren had ever seen a man with his head blown off.

January went by without incident. Day after day, night after night. The watches changing

120

every noon at the flagpole, the patrols going out, the flag still flying defiantly over the Bay's fort. The whole thing developed a kind of improbable tin-soldier air. But Nancy was over there. And she was real and always in his mind. When would all this end?

He got hold of Sally. "Tell me, Weasel, what's this secret way you have of getting in over there?"

"Oh, it's by the trading gate. Why? I wouldn't dare go over there now." Her eyes grew big. She dropped her voice to a whisper. "Are you going to rescue Nancy?"

"Like a princess in distress? No, Sally. But if I can get a message in, well. . ."

She told him about the post in the palisade that had rotted through at the bottom, and you could push it inwards just enough to squeeze through. He wrestled with the idea of somehow getting Nancy out, and plan after plan churned through his mind. None of them, though, could guarantee that she would not be shot by one side or the other.

Jo, the Iroquois, was sent up to Fort Chipewyan to take the news to Fergus Macdonald and to get a duplicate set of returns. It was important those reports reach Montreal as soon as possible. Ti'moine headed east with the Ile-à-la-Crosse returns without waiting for Jo to get back. He'd take them as far as Rapid River and they'd be relayed on from there.

In February they were both back. Jo brought word that the courier who had been killed was a Slave Indian known as Quick Feet. Jo and Ti'moine both joined Duncan's watch.

He was glad to have two good men like them. The others were dead bored by now and it was very hard to keep them on their toes — even Leo Bedard. Coco Pinet was far less than satisfactory in spite of his agile mind.

Coco had been plucked out of his comfortable duties as a messman in the bachelors' quarters because more men were needed for the patrols. Duncan twice caught him skulking around the kitchen when he should have been out on picket duty. "Only getting a little snack to take out to les gars, m'sieu. . . ."

Then he'd been all but asleep on watch, curled up in a snow shelter, with a flask of rum. Playing the fiddle and enjoying the limelight were more to Coco's taste.

"Once more, mon ami," Duncan growled at him, "and your pay for the winter is docked. Every sou."

The letters that came via Jo from Fergus Macdonald caused Angus Cameron to call a council. Duncan was shocked at the lines between his father's eyes and the greyness of his face. Worry. There must be a great deal on his mind. And his sickness. The whole supply of Turlington's Balsam was exhausted.

"There's trouble in the Athabasca too, gentlemen. We'd have heard about it sooner if our express had got through. It seems there was a fight with some Bay hunters over a moose. One

122

thing led to another and Mr. Macdonald drove the whole lot o' them out to fend for themselves for the winter. Men, women and children."

Duncan sucked in his breath.

"Good for him," Benson growled.

"Well," Cameron said, "my way may take a wee bit longer, Mr. Benson, but we'll spill no blood. We'll have them starved out in a month. Unless they mutiny before that."

Duncan took over the watch from Farquhar under the flagpole at noon on a raw overcast day. Farquhar unslung the big double-barrelled pistol in its holster which was daily passed from hand to hand. He presented it to Duncan with a flourish.

"Your badge of office, Sir Knight, and it's loaded. Speaking of nights, it promises to be a dark one, and schemes may be afoot. Beware!"

It was snowing heavily when Duncan headed out to check his pickets after dark. He followed Ti'moine's two-hour-old snowshoe tracks onto the lake and up into Back Bay. Farquhar was right, it was a good night for a breakout. Fresh tracks would be covered in an hour, and you couldn't see more than fifty yards. He still had some pain from his frozen foot and it slowed him down, especially on snowshoes. It might be wise to get more men out on patrol.

He cut through the alders and up onto the shore at the same place he'd met Nancy that Sunday morning. An age ago, it seemed. The track led onwards through scrubby thickets.

Snow muffled sound. You'd scarcely hear a musket shot a quarter mile away in this.

The first picket's tracks veered off to the right and Duncan turned that way. The men had built a string of lean-tos just inside the scrub. They could watch the fort's approaches in some kind of shelter.

The first of them loomed near. Visibility was getting worse. There'd be a real pile-up of snow before the night was over. At least it wasn't blowing. The second lean-to. No one inside. Another two hundred yards. The third.

"Hello. . ." A pair of snowshoes beside it, upright in the snow. "Hello." No reply. He crouched down.

"Inside there. Who's that?" Duncan reached into the blackness. He felt a leg, a body, a shoulder. "Come on then. No games." He shook hard.

"Heh?. . . Qui passe?. . ." A muffled voice, two-thirds asleep.

"Out of it. Come out." No reply. Only heavy breathing. And a whiff of rum.

Duncan found two moccasined feet. He grabbed them, heaved the prone figure out into the snow.

Who else but Coco Pinet?

"Heh, m'sieu. . ." His voice was thick. "Inside . . .just to keep a little warm. . .only five minutes, m'sieu. . . ." He half sat up, fumbled about.

Duncan spotted the flask, picked it up. "Here it is, clochard."

"Have a little drink, m'sieu."

"No, but it goes in my pocket, what's left. Up on your feet, Pinet. No more warnings for you." There was cold anger in his voice. He had the man by the front of his capote. "You're going to go back to the fort, find Mr. Maclaren and tell him I need four more men and that you're under arrest. You hear? And if you don't do that, you'll not only lose your winter's pay, I'll see you flogged and in the lock-up till spring. Understand?"

He could see Pinet's eyes bug. "Oui, m'sieu. Oui. No harm, m'sieu. I did no harm." The smell of rum was very strong. He fumbled for his snowshoes.

"You did nothing but sit in there drinking rum. Now you're no use to man or beast. That's the harm you've done. Now get on." The small figure lurched off through the dark. He'd even forgotten his musket.

"Damn!" Duncan shook his head. He'd have to cut through quickly to find Ti'moine now, reorganize the men, then head for the fort to meet the new lot and station them. No sleep tonight. . . .

He moved as fast as he could along the trail, cursing his foot and Coco Pinet. There was a slash pile ahead, and beyond that he could make out a stand of spruce. Then he saw new tracks.

They cut straight across his. Snowshoes. With a light toboggan. No sign of dogs. And going out, away from the fort. With this snowfall, they must be no more than five, ten minutes old. Oho!

He checked his musket. Half-cock and fresh primed. The pistol too.

He crossed a clearing, plunged along a path slashed through young willows. Fifty yards and it rose a little, then dropped towards a hollow, a clearing and a patch of skinny spruce. Over there. . . .

What was that? He stopped dead, looked again. By the spruce. Low down. Dark against the dark. A movement. Animal or. . .man?

He moved forward, very careful with his snowshoes. Thirty yards, twenty-five, no more. He dropped to one knee. It was moving. . . slightly. An easy shot. Yes. A man, crouched down, beside something. The toboggan? He raised his gun.

He'd never killed a man. He pulled full back on the cock, heard it click. He aimed. Right on the centre of the dark form. His finger tightened. He was going to. . .

Then he heard his own voice. "You! Stand. Raise your hands or I shoot you dead."

The dark figure froze. No sound. Only the silence of the snow.

"I mean it. Stand or I shoot."

Slowly the form ahead began to rise. He followed with his gun.

"Now raise your hands. . ."

Something to his right. Moving. Someone.

Ambush! He swung his gun.

Then, "It's Duncan. Don't shoot. *Don't. . .*" He flattened at the scream. Full length in the snow, steeling for the shot.

"Mother! No! It's Duncan Cameron." It was Nancy, shouting. Nancy Spence. Nancy that he'd nearly shot! And the other. . .

"Stand, Mr. Cameron. Without your gun." It had to be her mother, Jane. He rose slowly, breath rasping in his throat.

"Nancy, what's happening?" His eyes were still on the older woman. Her gun was at her shoulder.

"We're going out to our snares. Rabbits, birds. Whatever we can get." Nancy was close now.

"Those men send *you* out? Into this kind of danger? Do you know what can happen?"

"They're afraid. We come by our own will." Jane Spence's musket did not waver. Neither did her voice. "For my children and my husband. My children must not starve." It was as simple and direct as that.

He found his voice. "No one will starve if you just turn Whistler over."

"Whistler is in control." Nancy shook her head. "The Chipewyan got out past your men, we think. Whistler tells everyone there'll be relief from Fort Carlton any time. So they hold on."

"Nancy, you know he's a murderer."

She nodded. "But the others support him."

"For God's sake, don't challenge him then."

Even in this dim light he could see her face was drawn, her cheekbones sharp and gaunt. Her eyes were deep in hollows. Why should men be killed and children starve to death? For furs, of all things. Furs.

"Duncan, we have our snare lines. Will you let us go? Please?"

Getting out was one thing. They had managed it before. If they were caught coming back by someone else, though. . .two women. Revenge for the death of the courier. No!

"Come with me," he urged. "You'll be quite safe, I promise."

"My children." Jane Spence need say nothing more. Nancy's face was set.

"Then how long will you stay out?" He turned to Jane Spence. "Trust me, madame."

"Three days. More. We have far to travel. The weather too. The moon's nearly full."

"Come back on the third night from now, or the sixth or ninth." Duncan's words came tumbling out. "No other. I'll meet you exactly here at this same time and see that you get through."

He paused. "If you don't trust me, madame, you'd be better off to shoot me now."

Traitors were shot. Traitors.

She said, "I'll make the sound of an owl. . . twice."

She did so softly, and it hung eerily in the falling snow. "You call back the same way. Once if there's danger, three times if it's safe."

The sound of an owl. He cupped his hands, thumbs together, rounded his mouth, as he had when he was small. The sound came. Three times over.

It was no night for owls. Wind moaned in the poplar tops and the moon peered through a scudding layer of cloud. In the sudden brightness, he could see that no one had been through here since the heavy snow three nights before.

He crouched at the edge of the clearing, listening. A distant wolf's cry came riding down the wind. The trees cracked, brittle with the cold. Traitor. The word ran through his mind. He was a traitor. But he could do nothing less.

He had posted most of his men well round to the north. Ti'moine Tremblay was at the far end. Jo, the Iroquois, Leo Bedard and the youngest Favreau were stationed in between. Near Back Bay he'd posted Laframboise, who'd replaced Pinet.

The owl called clearly — twice.

He looked around. He stood, paused. Why wait? It was as safe as it would ever be. He slipped his mitts off, raised his hands. Three long calls. He waited. The shadows by the spruce were very deep. Above them the poplars clawed the ragged sky. He heard nothing but the wind and the rattling branches and the rustle of dry leaves on the birch.

The moon broke through the cloud, painting

the snow silver. Shadows lanced across it from the trees. The blackness of the spruce seemed even deeper. Then he saw them on the trail, moving slowly, very slowly. They were hunched over, one hauling the toboggan. The other, with a pole, pushing from behind. He stepped from the shadows.

They stopped and he drew close. Nancy barely breathed his name. Like her mother's, her face was haggard with fatigue.

"We killed a caribou," Jane said. There was no triumph in her voice. She was beyond that. It was a very heavy load. She eased the tumpline from around her head.

He said quickly, "No time to spare. I'll scout ahead and wait for you at the edge. One call for danger. Three for safe." He had to keep them moving. He turned and ran.

He broke through the edge of scrub. There stood the Hudson's Bay fort. A stark, black, distant rectangle on an empty moonlit plain. No light showed. The north wind plucked the alder, chased swirls of snow across the void.

He looked behind. A bank of cloud was racing from the west. It would blot out that brilliant moon. He made the signal, crouched and watched. Nothing moved out on that bleak expanse. Nothing. . . .

A gentle creak from the toboggan and they were there beside him. They huddled together, watching the cloud reach out to swallow up the moon. Like a shroud, cloud shadow raced across the wood, engulfed the snow, themselves.

"Go safely," he whispered.

Jane Spence leaned towards him and pressed her cold lips to his cheek. She stood slowly, then turned away, settling the tumpline around her hood.

He looked at Nancy. Words rushed out. "Stay with me," he said. "We'll go away. Like that Sunday with the dogs. Wherever you like. I want you to. . ."

She turned to him and shook her head. "Mother, my family, I must help them. And Father needs us all." Her eyes were dark shadows. He could barely hear her voice.

"And Whistler?" How could he speak the words? "Tell me, Nancy, are you Whistler's wife?"

"No," she said, "no, and I'll never be." She leaned towards him, brushed his cheek with dry cracked lips. "One day it will be over. Then come for me."

"Wherever you are," he said.

She moved behind the toboggan with her pole and began to push.

He watched them as they went, growing smaller, blending together, melting in the darkness. They must have a lookout in the watchtower. From up there, surely they would see. Someone would come out to help.

It brightened. He glanced up, cursing. The moon's cold face was crystal bright. The gap raced by. The cloud took over. But only for a minute, then more light. He could see them out there, less than halfway to the fort. Like some strange caterpillar creeping slowly on.

If he could see them, others could. Cloud. The cloud must come! They were moving. But so slow. So very slow. Beyond them the deeper darkness of the fort. He counted out the time. How long had they been gone? How far was it across? A wind-ripped rag of cloud cut down the light.

Then he saw another movement. Far off to the left. Clear of the brush. Two, three men. Stark in the moonlight. Running, with loping strides. Moving fast. Cloud shadow swept across, snuffed them out. They could only be his men. Ti'moine. Jo. They had seen the toboggan. They must have. They were going right for it. The darkness lingered. He could only dimly see the fort. Nothing else. He strained his eyes. Were they?. . .

The cloud curtain lifted. The scene burned acid deep in Duncan's mind. The toboggan. So slow. The fort behind. The racing men to the left, angling to cut them off. Like wolves running down a moose. They'd catch them. Yes, they would. The wolves would win.

He was on his feet and running, straight ahead. Blindly. Barely thinking. Knowing only that he had to stop his men. Stop them from doing what he had ordered them to do. He ran faster, faster. The gap was closing and the fort was closer. He could see the bastion and the watchtower now.

"Stop! Ti'moine, Jo, *stop*!" he bellowed.

Heads turned his way. They faltered, then ran on. His feet felt like lead. Like running in a dream. The toboggan had. . .how far to go?

The men were close now. He could see guns in their hands, capotes swinging, the upturns on their snowshoes, Ti'moine's streaming sash, his toque bobbing. Jo well ahead, feet flying. Someone else behind. Leo. The palisade loomed high. There was a spark of light up there. Away up.

"Jo, Ti'moine!" He screeched it out. "Stop, stop, stop." Only yards to go. The toboggan to his right was moving faster but the men were too close now. An easy shot.

Jo dropped to one knee, his musket up.

Then Duncan leaped. Flat out, he hit the kneeling Jo. The musket flew. Jo bellowed, heaved him half off. On his back now Duncan saw Ti'moine racing up, raising his own gun as he ran, straight at Duncan. He took him for an enemy. Of course. The moon was bright behind him. . . .

Suddenly, "Sacrement!" Ti'moine knew him. He stopped dead. His musket wavered. "Maudit." Disbelief in his voice. "M'sieu Cameron. . ." He ran on twenty more paces, stopped, his own gun up. Beyond him, Nancy and Jane Spence at the toboggan, trapped animals, waiting to be killed. They looked at Ti'moine, at the barrel of his musket.

Then the bastion above them erupted into sudden flame. The snow around Ti'moine was rent with shot. It ripped him, slammed him on his back. The thunder of the rampart gun, the bellowing of muskets battered Duncan's ears.

The dark figures with the toboggan picked up their step. They faded in the shadow of the palisade. The gate must have opened, for they simply disappeared. Ti'moine Tremblay lay still and silent on the snow.

Duncan heard low and bitter words. Inches from his face was Jo's. There was hatred in his eyes. No understanding. Only hatred and contempt. This boy who was their commander had robbed them of their quarry. He had warned their enemy. Worse, he had brought death upon their friend.

A traitor. He was a traitor. Now he knew the meaning of the dreadful word.

10
Exile

He crouched on that windswept plain for an eternity, his head down, his eyes shut, waiting — hoping — for the blast of gunfire that would snuff him out. He heard a voice shouting in his ear, felt a hand tug roughly at his shoulder. He turned and saw two figures running towards the distant line of scrub. Then he slowly rose, bracing for the shots to come. He walked to the pathetic bundle on the moon-bright snow, and knelt. Ti'moine was dead.

There were shouts up on the ramparts. Reloading? He didn't care. He gathered up the shattered body and it felt weightless in his arms. The blue of the capote was deeply stained with blood. He turned his back on the guns above and slowly walked away.

It was a bitter endless nightmare then. Shame swept over shame, like waves breaking on a cold deserted beach. Jo and Leo were silent. They stayed behind him on the long walk back, their muskets ready. Dawn came as they walked in through the gate.

Ti'moine's widow wailed. She sank to her haunches in the doorway and rocked, her children clustering around. How long before they knew who bore the blame? The women in their blankets gathered, ghostly in the half light, and the dirge swelled and grew. Hearts poured out their grief.

Men grouped in the shadows, murmuring the story mouth to mouth. Duncan walked away, across the square, a hundred pairs of eyes burning in his back. A light showed in a window of the Cameron house. . . .

"Betrayal. There is no other word. Spence's wife and daughter. . . . Women, starving children notwithstanding. . . . No." Angus Cameron's eyes were anguished. His head kept on shaking, slowly shaking. "There is no other word. So I have to ask myself, Mr. Cameron, what would I do if you were no kin o' mine?"

"Whatever, sir, then please do it." Duncan looked straight back. His eyes were hollow, his face drained. "A good man died because of me. I don't ask consideration."

Bagpipes started the wrenching, sad lament and matched the keening voices of the women. Farquhar paced slowly near the gate. Duncan could see him from the window. And the crowd of men, silent, close-knit, stared at the house from across the square.

As the day lightened, Favreau marched out, stumpy, resolute, straight to the bare flagpole. He bent the folded flag to the halyard and hoisted it to the top. It snapped in the icy wind. He

136

lowered it half-mast and stood looking straight at the bourgeois' door.

His actions spoke. The men out there wanted to know the bourgeois' decision. Young Cameron could not stay forever in the sanctuary of the house. Sooner or later he must step out there. Into the yard.

"My husband." Rose Flower's voice was urgent. She spoke in Cree and Duncan strained to understand. "I must go to mourn with Tremblay's widow. Then I will ask her for forgiveness for my son and make a gift to her of all I own. If she accepts, her family may let the matter rest."

"Even if I would allow that," Cameron shook his head, "it would not satisfy the men."

He looked out the window and said evenly, "And it would not satisfy justice. No, he must answer for this himself. I cannot allow you to beg of Tremblay's widow."

"I beg for my own son," she said in English, and her eyes snapped. Then she whirled out the door and walked erect across the square to Ti'moine's door.

The mourning went on all day and through the night. In the grey forenoon, with the wind sighing fitfully, Angus Cameron stood beneath the half-mast flag and read from his prayer book in a hard flat voice: "Ashes to ashes, dust to dust. . ."

Favreau intoned in half-remembered Latin. The men muttered prayers, fingering their rosaries. They finished with the sign of the cross.

The women were not there. They stayed clustered at the widow's house where they had lit a fire for burning offerings. Bare-headed, Duncan stood apart, the cold wind's fingers reaching deep inside.

He watched as the coffin was carried shoulder high out through the gate to the sad slow march of Farquhar's pipes. It was followed by every man, woman and child.

He remained in the square, head bowed, and he was utterly alone.

Favreau had always kept a cool distance from Duncan. It was not his place to be friendly with his bourgeois' son. Neither was he a friend of Angus Cameron. He had a deep and abiding respect for him, though, built on many years together. He understood the problem that he faced.

Gavin Farquhar told Duncan later how Favreau had gathered all the canoemen and artisans right under the platform where the coffin would rest until the spring.

"True," he said to them, "young M'sieu Cameron permitted those two women to pass by. He must answer to le grand bourgeois himself. You and me, we cannot judge. If he had not stopped Jo and Leo, they too might be dead. And he played the man. He offered his own life to get Ti'moine — with the cannon just up there." He gestured and looked straight in every eye. "How many here would do the same?"

There was a long silence, then the shuffling of moccasins on the snow. Leo Bedard looked at his feet. The muscles in Jo's face twitched and tightened.

Later, in front of all the clerks in the mess, Peter Maclaren ordered Duncan confined to his room.

"I will lock the door and hold the key myself," he said primly, suppressed triumph in his eyes, "and send you your meals and an escort to the privy."

"Locked doors? Escort?" It was Gavin Farquhar who spoke up. "Sir! Just ask for his parole. Any gentleman. . ."

"Gentleman?"

"Aye, sir. Gentleman." There was unexpected steel in Farquhar's voice. "If you are so little a gentleman yourself that you want another bond, I'll give it."

Lips compressed, Maclaren eyed Farquhar. Then he nodded curtly and left the room. Young Cameron, after all, was no longer any threat to his prospects of a partnership. And he could even up with Farquhar.

Angus Cameron sent for Duncan. "Favreau has put to me a submission from the men that you should not be treated as a traitor. Your mother says that the widow finds understanding in her heart. But you must leave right away. I cannot keep you here."

"I understand, sir."

"Those canoemen are fickle, easily swayed. But I must tell you direct, I myself can find no

139

mitigation for what you've done." His father looked grey faced and ill, but his voice was hard as steel. "No gentleman, sir, would betray his trust as you did."

Was that what cut the deepest? Or was it the knowledge that Ti'moine Tremblay's happy life had been snuffed out because of him?

"So you're no longer employed by the North West Company, or by Cameron and Letellier. Within twenty-four hours you'll leave."

Rose Flower sat motionless by the fire. Duncan knelt beside her and she turned her eyes to his. They were sad with loss. "My son, go to my father's tent, west of Lac la Ronge. He is called Cut Hand. . . ." He could find refuge there with her family — his family.

"I'll ask his blessing, Mother," Duncan said, "but I must make my way alone."

Angus Cameron made two concessions. He wrote him a licence to trade independently two hundred miles to the east, on the far side of Lac la Ronge. There was a small establishment at the mouth of Hunter Bay that had not been used for several years. Also he could buy trade goods to the amount of his back pay on the company's books.

A good part of his money, though, went to Ti'moine's widow — via Gavin Farquhar, who staunchly helped him through. He bought eight dogs from her, a set of harness and a working toboggan for twice what they were worth. Now with her inheritance from Ti'moine and the

140

wealth from Rose Flower, she would have no difficulty finding another husband.

There was puzzlement and hurt in Sally's face when he went to the Cameron house to say good-bye.

"Sally, speak to Nancy when you can. Tell her I'll be at Lac la Ronge. Ask her when this is over to get word to me and I'll come. Someday." He did his best to smile.

"Someday, Duncan?" The tears welled in her eyes.

"Wherever she may be."

His mother's eyes held sadness, love and deep understanding. She said little but she held him close. His father wasn't there. Then he walked across the square and every single back was turned. Except for Gavin Farquhar's. He was at the gate to say good-bye.

Duncan left Ile-à-la-Crosse with a loaded toboggan, urging his fractious dogs along the open bleakness of the lake. At its end he would pass the Shagwenaw Rapid and follow the chain of lakes and linking river that formed the eastward-flowing Missinippe. Cloud was gathering to the west. There'd be more snow. He looked back once across the miles of even white at the dwindling forts — those two dark stains along the whiteness of the distant shore. Two log-walled bastions of. . .what?

"Hike hike hike. Belle, get along the trail. Get on. Fripon, Ti'bleu, marche. . ."

11
Spring

'The establishment' at Hunter Bay turned out to be four walls filled with snow and the collapsed remnant of a roof — a forlorn sight at the end of his long journey. It was a lonely spot, on a rocky point with an endless white horizon to the west. He had only his dogs as companions, but now they knew each other well. A week together on the trail and each understood the others' foibles. It was a comforting morning ritual to talk to them, to rough their heavy coats and scratch their ears and feel their glad response. It took a week's steady work to put the place in livable shape, and it was about then that his first visitor arrived.

He came in through the islands from the west, running with four dogs and a light load. Lean and quiet, he hunkered down beside the fire for tea. Eventually he spoke.

"Cut Hand, the Canoe-maker, lives across the big lake and two more beyond that. He sends a welcome to the son of his daughter, Rose Flower, and of his friend, Crooked Nose." He opened his pack and brought out two fine marten skins and a glossy beaver. "Cut Hand would like to trade with you."

"I'll be honoured to come to Cut Hand's tent," Duncan said, struggling with his Cree. "Will you show me the way?"

There was a pause for tea. "Cut Hand will come to you. Soon. He's not far off." Another long silence. "I'm the son of his younger brother. Some call me Silent Partridge."

Duncan found the Cree for 'my cousin.' Silent Partridge repeated it back, smiled and they shook hands. He left with tobacco and two knives as gifts for Cut Hand and himself.

Next day he re-appeared with a taller man, six dogs and a strangely bulky load. Duncan had time to change to his fur coat and best gloves and moccasins and open up his trade packs before they pulled in. On top of the heavy load was a fourteen-foot canoe.

The imposing figure with Silent Partridge could be no one but his grandfather, Cut Hand. He stood tall and straight, with a lean hawk's face and deep-set eyes. He wore a hat of lynx, with the mask of the animal set nose down on his forehead and the tufted ears erect. It added to his height and gave him an outlandish, even fierce appearance. The lines clustered at the corners of his eyes, though, spoke of kindness and laughter.

His coat too was of lynx, and it was identical to Duncan's. So were the patterns and the colours on his moccasins. He took off his mitts, leaving them dangling by their strings. On his left hand only the thumb and index finger remained.

"I see Crooked Nose in your face and in the way you stand," the old man said. "I see my daughter Rose Flower in your eyes. We shall see, my grandson, what is in your heart."

He reached out and took Duncan's hands in his.

The canoe was a thing of beauty. Light and strong and of perfect symmetry. It was made of a very big sheet of bark — rare this far to the north — cut in late summer and mellowed to a golden brown. Etched near the bow was a representation of a lynx. It had been made especially for him.

Duncan's gift seemed unimportant beside it — a silver-handled ceremonial dirk which he had bought. . .how long ago?. . .from a silversmith in Montreal.

Though Cut Hand asked no questions, Duncan felt compelled to tell him haltingly how he had been banished by his father. But the old man gently raised his hand. "I know enough of that. Give yourself no further pain."

The furs they brought to trade were the finest Duncan had ever seen. Cut Hand sat back, smiling faintly as Duncan and Silent Partridge settled the price on each skin. Then he watched Duncan measuring out powder, weighing tobacco and shot, selecting axe heads and lance points.

He nodded. "Like your father, you bargain firmly and you give good measure."

Duncan sent with him a present of tea and a kettle for his grandmother, Snow Bird. As he watched his grandfather and Silent Partridge disappear across the lake, he no longer felt so utterly alone.

Spring stirred restless in his blood. The warming of the land, the thawing of the snow, the singing of frogs and the cries of countless geese. . .that yearning in the chest, that reaching out for new beginnings. The aching wish that certain things might be different than they were.

As soon as the lake was open, Cree canoes brought furs to Hunter Bay, and the women had some clothes to sell. They could have gone another thirty miles to the North West Company's post at the mouth of Rapid River but Cut Hand's influence guided them to Duncan. No one was disappointed with the trading.

There was no news, though, from Ile-à-la-Crosse. The outcome of the siege? What had been resolved? And Nancy? Had the Spences left? Where had they gone? And what of Whistler? They might know something at the Rapid River post and the spring brigades would soon pass down.

Deep-loaded with six heavy packs of furs, Duncan paddled north along the wooded rock-bound shore. The rich tanned smell of his new skin clothes filled his nostrils. His hair was long now and tied behind. He could have been one of his own Cree family going down to trade.

The alder and the willow showed yellow-green. The faintest new-leaf colour spread among the poplar and the birch. A purplish haze lay upon the rounded hills. The breeze played gently on his cheek and his back warmed luxuriously in the morning sun.

His canoe handled as beautifully and moved as swiftly as it had promised. The lake contracted to a river. Water swirled among the alders, moving high and fast and full. Shores narrowed towards a rapid far too wild in high water to run safely in his small canoe. He portaged two packs at a time, then paddled on in the outrace, eddies plucking at his blade.

He slipped in silence through five miles of open lake. It lay like glass, the late day sun behind. A loon cried, exultant for its mate. Ducks came in through long shadows, wings hammering, then touched down — audible in the stillness miles away.

Long before he reached Nistowiak, he could hear its thunder and see the high-hung cloud of spray. It rose like some ghostly figure from the blackness of the forest, shifting and swaying, blood-reddened by the last rays of the setting sun.

The water from the south leaped outwards here in a mighty arc, plunging to a twisted gorge

146

below. It thundered in his ears. He could feel its awesome power. The half-mile portage path was smoothed by the age-old passage of migrating feet. It passed through fragrant, giant trees. They were hung with moss. They dripped with spray. They shut away the evening sky.

At the bottom, where the river rushed to join the mighty Missinippe on its journey east, he made his camp. It was a place his ancestors had used for countless years. Right across the darkening swirl a light marked out the Rapid River post.

In the morning he would go across and trade.

Ian Dawson, the Post Master, was carefully polite. He was on the main canoe route and he had met Duncan on the stop-over here last fall. It was strange for him to re-appear alone, dressed in common buckskin, but Dawson contained his surprise.

"Tell me now, Mr. Cameron, and how goes the battle at Ile-à-la-Crosse?"

"Battle?"

"Aye. We did hear from the winter express courier about the Indian who was killed and the siege. Tremblay, was it, who came through?. . ." He turned to his interpreter, a reddish-haired half-breed with quick eyes and a limp.

He nodded. "A good man, Ti'moine Tremblay."

"Tremblay too is dead." The words jerked from Duncan's lips. Dead. The sound echoed and re-echoed in his ears.

"Dead?. . ."

"Yes." He felt worse than callous. "Now look at these foxes. . ."

"You got these from Lac la Ronge? Cut Hand and his people?" Dawson's eyes narrowed. He knew he'd have to pay more for furs that had gone through another's hands. If only he'd gone out during the winter. . .

He was tough with his trading. No one got favours. He was on a percentage of the profit from his post. But these were prime furs. He had to pay. The interpreter advised him quietly. Two women stayed much in the background, preparing food.

"The brigade should be down any day, Mr. Cameron. You'll be welcome to bide here."

"I think not, thank you. I'll leave a letter for Angus Cameron, though, if you would oblige."

"You're very busy then at Hunter Bay?" Dawson frowned his puzzlement. "Must you race back without seeing your, ah. . .father?"

"I'll camp on the other side. Wouldn't put you to any trouble." He had no wish to fend off probing questions. Besides, he preferred to be alone.

He'd made a good profit on his trading. It was a step towards independence. If he heard from Nancy, maybe he could bring her here. Soon there would be news. Surely there'd be news. . . .

In two days the canoes came sweeping down

the river, their vermilion paddles flashing in the morning sun. The lead canoe, for some reason, came his way, towards the mouth of Rapid River. The others sheered off towards the post.

He heard the singing, then he saw old Favreau in the bow. It was le grand bourgeois' canoe. He stayed concealed, well back among the trees. There was Angus Cameron's tall hat. And someone else. Another figure, half concealed. Benson? Farquhar? Who?. . .

Then he saw them. All of them. The whole family. In the canoe with Cameron. His mother, Sally, Raymond, Cat, the baby.

The canoe ran to the portage. Two voyageurs were over in an instant, waist deep, holding it clear of the rocks. Then two more were in the water, offering their backs — first to their grand bourgeois, then Madame and then the children. The small ones jumped down from their pick-a-back, delighted. Packs and baggage were briskly passed ashore, and in seconds the canoe was high on two strong shoulders heading up the path.

His own family. All of them. Going through to Lac la Ronge?

No point skulking in the bush. He stepped out. Favreau saw him first and froze. The other men stopped. A growl from Favreau and they turned away, slung up their packs and trotted after the canoe.

"Duncan!" his brother Raymond shouted and dashed for him. "You're an Indian, Duncan."

Cat followed, laughter on her face. Duncan knelt, arms wide, and caught them as they ran.

"We're going to stay with you. At Lac la Ronge. We're going to stay with Duncan. We're going to stay with Duncan." They sang it in his ears.

Duncan looked up into Sally's smiling face, and at his mother's — lit with pleasure. Angus Cameron looked grey. His face was deeply lined. His arms stayed folded and he made no move to greet his son.

"I fear there may be more violence up at Ile-à-la-Crosse," he said. "I believe they'll be safer near Cut Hand. Favreau will take them through to Hunter Bay. Then he'll catch up with me."

"Mother says her whole family's summer gathering is at Lac la Ronge," Sally said. "We'll stay till Father comes back in the fall."

His mother said, "I wish to be with you and near my people — our people — while my husband is away."

"That's wonderful, wonderful."

"And Duncan. Duncan." Raymond tugged at Duncan's sleeve. "We burned the Hudson's Bay fort down." He looked proudly at his brother and his eyes were huge. "It burned and burned."

"Burned it down?" Duncan choked on the words. Nancy. What about Nancy?

Cat began to chant. "Ladybug, ladybug, fly away home. Your house is afire and your children will. . ."

"Cat!" Sally stopped her sharply.

"You burned it down!" Duncan flung the words at Angus Cameron's wintry face. "What happened, sir, what happened to. . .everyone there?"

"Whistler slipped away in late March. Escaped. Spence surrendered the whole of his establishment in return for safe passage south to Edmonton House for all his people. We took Spence's stock and burned the place to the ground."

Then at least Nancy should be safe. But her father would be leaving soon for home. Where would she go then? Somewhere along the Saskatchewan? Edmonton? Carlton House? Cumberland? And Whistler? What about Harry Whistler? Sally might know.

Cameron turned to his wife. "Will you walk the children to the top, please, my Bonnie. I'll talk with Duncan."

Climbing the steep pull, he had to shout over the roar of the water. "It's an eye for an eye now. The Bay are fighting back. And the chances are I might not return this fall. I have furlough overdue, and with the stones. . . I'll write from Fort William after I've seen the doctor there. If I go out for surgery, the best place for her ladyship and the bairns is right here near her own. Including you."

He stopped at the top above the falls and turned to Duncan. "The trading licence you have is only for the season, you understand. I'll have to put it before the council in Fort William. If they don't approve. . .well, at least you can stay on at Hunter Bay, and I can send a credit up to Dawson so you can look after things."

"Father, what if. . .well, the surgery. . ." Duncan couldn't finish.

"What if I don't come back, you mean?" Cameron's voice was harsh. "What if I die? Well, I've made a will. There's good provision. And there's school for the children. The Letelliers will look after them. Your mother can choose where she wants to live."

"She'd want to be with the children surely."

"In Montreal?" Cameron frowned. He looked over at the three of them playing by the canoe, the cradle-board propped up, with the baby watching. The voyageurs were squatted with their pipes some way along the shore. He said, "It would be up to her."

Rose Flower was kneeling at the edge of the falls, on the great slab of rock that overhung the water's plunge. She had lit a fire, and it occurred to Duncan that she must have brought her own dry wood to this spray-drenched place. Smoke rose around her and mingled with the shifting cloud.

He watched his father, bare-headed, go and crouch beside her. He saw the two of them take each other's hands, talk for a time. Then he held her close and rose. He looked down at her, at the fire, at the water and the smoke and the spray, and at last he turned away.

He came and hugged his three young children. Then he spoke to Duncan, and his voice was hard as steel. "Now, sir, can I depend on you to care for your own kin?"

"You can, sir." How could he question that? Duncan swallowed his sudden anger. "You can, indeed."

They watched Angus Cameron stride, straight-backed, down the portage path until he was swallowed by the trees.

Duncan felt a sudden stabbing sense of loss. Would they ever come to know each other now? Out on the rock his mother dropped something in the fire. The smoke changed. It grew darker and thickened, and it rose up to join the lingering spray. She bowed her blanket-covered head.

An offering — it must be that — for her husband's safe return.

12
Lac la Ronge

Duncan and Sally sat on the rock below the cabin in the murmuring dusk. They hugged their knees and watched the swallows wheeling and darting after flies. Now and then one brushed the water, feather-light, to start a circle widening on the glassy lake. Loons began to call and their voices echoed in the stillness round and round the bay.

"I'm glad Mr. Favreau's gone, Duncan," she said. "You don't like to speak to each other, do you?"

"Favreau saved my skin back at Ile-à-la-Crosse. But he did it for Father. You see, he believes I was wrong. Father does too. I can understand it, but I can't undo it."

"Can't you come back home with us then?" She put her hands on one of his. "Ever?"

"Only if. . ." He shook his head and stopped himself. He had nearly said, 'Only if Father wants me back.' He went on. "Not for a while, Sally. I think this is home for me — for now."

"All by yourself?" She smoothed her skirt, her eyes down. "If this is home, are you going to have a wife?"

"Oh, no, not yet." He found a pebble and flicked it into the water. He glanced at Sally's profile. Her face had firmed. She was growing up, getting very pretty. Soon she'd be that age herself.

"Good. I think Nancy. . ."

"You saw her, Sally! You spoke?"

Sally nodded. "I sneaked over to their camp before they left," she whispered. Teasing now, she fished slowly in the pockets of her skirt. "Father said not, but I had to see Charlotte. And Nancy. She gave me this." She drew out a folded paper, held it up like a prize for a guessing game. "She knew you'd gone away. I told her you were here."

The note was sealed with wax. In her square, firmly printed hand, Nancy wrote:

> Duncan, There is too much for me to say. I must help my family. I will write when I know where we are going. Do not try to come before you hear from me. With love,
> Nancy

He could see her face, feel her strength and warmth. Yearning overtook him once again. For a long time he looked out at the faint line of the horizon, where the sun had sunk into the waters of the lake, blood red. Where was she in this endless land, in all this vastness? Where?

'I must help my family,' she had said. Did that mean Whistler? He tried to push him from his mind. Would he hear from her again? Should he just wait, or should he try to find her?

In the stillness he could hear Rose Flower in the cabin crooning to baby Malcolm. The other children were there too. They were in his charge, all of them. They were his responsibility. So that decided it. With them here, he could not go.

Sally echoed his own thoughts. "It's so very big. How could you ever find. . .anyone. Imagine if someone wanted to hide. You'd never, ever find them — like that Mr. Whistler or Coco Pinet."

"Coco Pinet?"

"He ran off, you know. Oh, that was after you left. Yes. He was locked up in the cell and Gavin Farquhar found all sorts of things he'd stolen. He'd hidden them away, like a magpie."

"And he escaped?"

"Yes." She nodded. "And he was so cheery, Coco. Such a marvellous fiddler too."

The crooning had stopped. The baby must be asleep.

Summer. The lake shimmered. Net floats bobbed off the mouth of the river which, for their own strange reason, the white men called the 'Montreal.' Teepees of Cree families clustered there. Fires burned. Drying racks and canoes were arrayed along the shore. The people — a good five hundred of them — had made long journeys to gather for the summer here, for their happy time. The Camerons came too, in answer to the invitation from Cut Hand.

The great encampment was alive with the sound of children shouting on the shore, and happy laughter, and barking dogs, and women scolding. It smelled of poplar smoke, curing fish and rotting guts, tanning hides and wet dogs and people. It surrounded them, enveloped them. And Duncan remembered it from some time long ago.

Cut Hand greeted them. "My daughter, my grandchildren, sons and daughters of Crooked Nose, welcome to my tent." Everyone gathered to welcome them too, to admire their splendid clothes, and to see father and daughter embrace.

Rose Flower seemed to soften. Her shoulders grew more supple, her back less rigid. Duncan had never seen her smile more warmly. Her liveliness and laughter returned. She was once more with her own.

Sitting cross-legged on the fresh-cut spruce next to the only grandmother he had known, Duncan heard the echo of her soft-spoken words of long ago. Tales of the legendary wiskedjak and of the wendigo, raven and mother moon, told in the smoky dimness of the teepee. She had seemed to him so ancient, even then. Now she was wizened and shrunken and she moved with care. Her eyes were clouded and she peered closely at each face. But she was as timeless and as loving as the land. She held her youngest grandchild in her arms, rocking him slowly, her voice a summer breeze singing in the pines.

Duncan gave her tobacco and tea and the medallion he had for her. It was pierced silver in the image of her own name — Snow Bird. Her clawed old fingers caressed it lovingly. She kissed her grandson's cheek, and he hung the medallion around her neck.

She had made clothing for each of them, but the gift she gave to Duncan was special. It was a glengarry cap — the wedge-shaped kind so many Scotsmen wore. It was made of heavy melton cloth bought from a trader, and it was encrusted with tiny beads. They were arranged in swirling, intertwined designs of flowers, birds and trees. How had her dim old eyes and crippled fingers done it? She placed it on his head and her pleasure reached out to all those there to share.

Proud Scot. Eternal Cree. He stemmed equally from both. Was he either? Was he neither? Was he both?. . .

Time stood still in the camp. Day followed contented day. Cut Hand had a good supply of bark, and he started a tiny hunting canoe for Raymond. The boy would learn to paddle — once he had helped in the building. Food was plentiful. Always fish when the nets were hauled, duck's eggs from the marshes, and gull's from the islands well offshore. Lazy days of gossiping, adjusting territories for the hunt, arranging marriages.

The sky for a time was hazed with the smoke of distant fires. Shad flies layered the surface of the lake until the wind came back and washed them under. Currants, rose hips, then blueberries all ripened. Children vied to bring the most.

Contentment? For everyone, perhaps, but Duncan. Restlessness gnawed. He was forever watching. Up the river. Out across the lake. Where? When? He would haul nets, then paddle long miles to the island to feed his dogs, going hard all day. He picked berries with the children, swam naked with them, brown and glistening on the beach. He gambled with the men and listened to their hunting talk, their disdainful jokes of white men.

The drums began, the singing and the dancing. Cut Hand in his finest clothes, his headdress, his calumet and feathered staff spoke eloquently of the land and family bonds. He led the men and older boys in their opening dance. Then the women started, lavishly dressed, jingling with their bells. Rose Flower, Sally, Raymond, Cat, all dressed in skin, danced with them. Slow rhythmic shuffling steps, with chanted words.

For ceremonial dress Duncan put on his Montreal grey suit and wore his beaded cap. He sat cross-legged and watched and listened.

Day. Night. Drums, dancing, speeches, song, smoking, talk. And the fires and the drums —

steadily, endlessly beating out their ancient sound.

He was on the fringe, reaching out to understand. He felt something reaching for him too. His mother, brothers, sisters — they had been embraced. But he could not quite respond.

He attracted many eyes. There were young women who dressed especially for his attention — ear bobs, hawk bells around their ankles, vermilion on their cheeks, rich embroidery on their clothes. Their glances, their invitations, were direct. They were lovely, fresh and vital, but they were not for him.

"Grandfather. . ." He watched the firelight play on Cut Hand's face on a cool late-summer night. Above the old man's head the sky was laced with shooting stars. "I must go back to Hunter Bay. My father left my mother and the children in my charge. So I should take them too."

Cut Hand put a stick in the fire and watched the tiny sparks. "We will miss you. Summer is the time for ease and the enjoyment of oneself and one another."

"I have to build a new cabin and a wall."

"As is the white man's way." Amusement showed in the wrinkles around his eyes. "Who would you keep out?"

"The English from the Bay may attack once they know we're here. You know of the troubles at Ile-à-la-Crosse. They say this land is theirs."

"Just as your father and the men from

160

Montreal say that it belongs to them?" Cut Hand shook his head and smiled. "How is land possessed? One may use a part of it, sufficient for a family's needs. Use it wisely in one's lifetime, then leave it as it was. But it's not possessed."

Duncan bowed his head to the fire. "You're right, Grandfather. But our. . .their ways are different."

"It has always been so." His eyes reflected untold years. "But your mother and the children, they'll be safe with me until the hunt. There are many hunters here in summer and they're well armed." He frowned. "Your father trusts his most precious possession to your care, yet you yourself are not welcome in his tent. That must one day be healed."

"That's my greatest wish."

"But, Grandson," his tone lightened, "you'll stay at Hunter Bay with none to help? None to fish and cook? And make the clothes you need for winter? And feed you? A man should have a wife. You're young, but you're rich enough. There are many fine girls here. I'll speak for you."

Duncan said, "My thanks, Grandfather, but I am. . .promised."

Cut Hand inclined his head. It was a man's own affair.

Leaving, Duncan could see that his mother and the young children had absorbed completely amongst the people. But not Sally. No, not quite.

Without asking, Silent Partridge and his woman, their baby and young son came with

161

him in their own canoe. The west wind chased them like scraps of cloud across the deep blue vastness, sliding through the rolling whitecaps streaked with foam. He could rarely see the other canoe among the hissing waves. It took a full day for them to get to Hunter Bay.

Duncan and Silent Partridge worked well together and his mischievous, shaggy-headed little boy was a surprisingly steady helper. By early fall the new cabin with storehouse attached and a strong palisade were complete.

It would soon be time to bring the dogs back in, and the cool brisk days and chill nights were right for drying stick fish for their winter feed.

Cut Hand brought Sally over to help with the endless tasks that prepared the way for winter. She worked happily, chattering away with Silent Partridge's woman, whom he called Laughing One. She tended the baby too, missing her own tiny brother. But soon the brigades would be coming up the Missinippe and they'd go to meet them at the Rapid River post. Their father would be back. As the time neared, Sally's excitement grew. But as each day passed, it was tainted more and more with nagging fears.

They sat close to the fire with the night-hawks thrumming outside and a wolf chorus sounding from the distant dark. She let her fears out with a sudden rush. "Father will come back, Duncan, won't he?"

162

He said, "Of course he will."

"But Mr. Spence isn't coming back, and Leo Bedard's turned off his wife and gone home. And Mr. Pringle. . ."

"Sally, Father's not the same."

Her face, her voice, were taut. "Well, over there at the summer camp some women say he'll not come back. They say he'll take another woman in his homeland. They say Mother should have another husband from among the Cree. I've heard them. I've heard them talk."

"Look, Father isn't well. He has these stones. The surgeon may have to cut them out. If he's not with the brigade this fall, we'll get a letter from him. Then he'll be back next year." He put his arm around her. "Come on, Weasel. Those women — it's silly gossip. Don't pay any heed."

He stretched out on a bearskin with his blankets. Sally had the newly built bunk. He dozed and her words conjured pictures in his mind. Their father, marrying some elegant lady. In a huge cathedral with a glorious fanfare — horses, carriages, toasts in champagne, ladies glittering with jewels, the great organ thundering out, a thousand candles and the choir's voices spiralling upwards to the vaulted heights. . . .

He half woke with the fire flickering on the underside of the low scoop roof. In the morning Sally was curled up close beside him, her small hand clutching his.

13
Fall

When the leaves had turned, they left Silent Partridge and his family at Hunter Bay and paddled to the Rapid River post. At the top of the Nistowiak portage, Sally changed into the print dress and matching bonnet which had been folded away neatly in her pack. She came out of the brush happily swirling her skirt. The bodice was very tight. Her little-girl figure was changing.

"Why, Madame," Duncan laughed. "Such a fine lady certainly can't carry a pack. Allow me!" He wore a fringed skin shirt with Cat's coloured sash, and leggings tied below the knee. His hair was long enough now to be braided at the back.

"Certainly, my man," she said haughtily. Then: "You know, you do look like Grandfather, Duncan."

"Thank you, Weasel," he laughed, "but you'd never talk to him that way, would you?"

From the bottom of the portage they could see Cut Hand's tent, gleaming in the golden sun, pitched not far from Dawson's post. Their mother would be there, and the others. Raymond and Cat came running down to meet them.

"We're going home, Duncan," sang Cat. "Going home. Are you coming home too? Come see Grandmother." Even bent old Snow Bird had come to say good-bye. There was no mail. No company canoes had yet arrived.

Dawson was less than civil to Duncan this time. He had obviously heard the whole tale from Ile-à-la-Crosse. He looked with outright scorn at the clothes Duncan wore, and at his beaded cap. What gentleman would not be dressed, as he was, in his best suit and tall beaver for the arrival of the brigades?

He had invited Madame Cameron and her younger children to stay inside the post, of course, but she preferred the teepee with her people. Two days of clear weather and frosty nights went by. Sally scanned the river with Duncan's small telescope screwed to her eye.

"Canoes. Look! Canoes!" He saw her dashing with the others to the shore. He stayed in the teepee with Snow Bird, watching through the flap. If his father asked for him, so be it. If not. . .

Each canoe paused to toss out a single pack, then forged straight on. The voyageurs doffed their caps and called friendly greetings to Rose Flower and the children — the bourgeois' family once again. They waved back happily.

Benson stepped ashore from the fourth canoe.

He bowed, handed Madame a large package and stood turning his hat in his hands. The children clustered close around their mother. Duncan saw Benson shake his head. No, Ma'am. He could almost hear the blunt voice: Mr. Cameron would not be coming home to Ile-à-la-Crosse. Not this year.

Benson bowed again, turned quickly. His canoe pulled out. They stood looking at the river, a forlorn little group in last year's Montreal clothes. No, Angus Cameron would not be coming home.

Duncan joined them in their silence by the shore. He cut the oilcloth package and took out his father's letter. It was addressed to 'Duncan Cameron Esq.' With Sally's help, he read it out in Cree.

> . . . .I write from Fort William just before I leave for Montreal. Dr. McLoughlin has confirmed that I must have surgery so I will go to Montreal and then to Edinburgh. Tell your mother please not to be concerned. I will return next spring in full health, and I will be back to Ile-à-la-Crosse with the brigade in the fall. . . .

"He's coming back, he is," Sally breathed. She wanted so much to believe it. Duncan saw the tears glistening in his mother's eyes.

> It should now be perfectly safe at Ile-à-la-Crosse, unless you have heard otherwise. Your mother and the children can go up

with Fergus Macdonald. He will be following Benson. . . .

Rose Flower put her hand on Duncan's arm. She slowly shook her head. "No, we'll stay at Hunter Bay."

. . . .Raymond Letellier is here for the partners' meeting. He has arranged places in school for both Sally and wee Raymond a year from now. Peter Maclaren will be coming to Fort William next spring and he will bring them down. I look forward to a fortnight with them before they go on to Montreal.

"School. It said me too." Raymond's eyes were wide. "It said me too."

. . . .You will be glad to hear that the partners have confirmed your trading licence and have extended it a year. You should know that Raymond Letellier spoke strongly for you, which I believe swung the deciding votes. With that in mind, you may wish to be in Fort William next year to make your own case. . . .

The deciding votes. It was a near thing then. Not promising for the future. He could see himself facing that council of flint-hard partners, explaining his actions. More important, convincing them he could make money for the company.

He could hear the private talk too, over cigars, between the council sessions: "These young bits o' brown, you know"..."Even Cameron's boy" ..."Raised by Letellier too — almost one of his own"..."Unreliable — so often seems to be the way, ye ken, with half-breeds...."

He looked at the river mirroring the whiteness of bare birch and tall spruce and a kingfisher flashing in the mellow noon-day sun, and he wondered just how important all that really was.

"Go on, Duncan."

There were messages for all the children and, of course, 'for my Bonnie.' There was a new volume of Robert Burns' poems and songs for Duncan, and Aesop's Fables with lovely coloured pictures 'for my Sally,' and a farmyard picture book 'to read to the wee ones.'

A note inside the Burns said, 'Duncan, I am no hand at poetry. Please read the verses starting on page 29 to your mother for me.'

The other package was addressed to him in a familiar hand. It held a morocco-bound edition of Molière's plays in two volumes. Both were inscribed warmly, 'Mon cher ami — Duncan Cameron. For company on long winter nights in the far North West,' and signed 'Marianne' with a cross for a kiss. Scatterbrain! She had given him those books before. He must write to thank her. But what else would he say? About Nancy? About his future and where it lay?

None of them wanted to stay here, where they had received bad news. They packed up

168

quickly, paddled their canoes across and climbed the portage. The sun was low. It was dark here beneath the trees. Sombre, with the giant trunks reaching up. Like a cathedral. The thunder of the falls grew stronger as they climbed.

Sally joined her mother with the children and Snow Bird and Cut Hand out at the edge of the cataract. She had her own small bundle of dry wood. Duncan watched her as she knelt with the water rushing past. Flint, fire-steel, tinder, puff of smoke. She bent to it, working up a clear and smokeless flame. Then came the offerings, something from each of them for the spirit of this place, burned in the fire.

Night fell early now. Cut Hand sniffed the wind and led them off their route to find a sheltered spot to camp. In the morning it was overcast and cold and blowing hard from the northeast. Across the grey streaked rollers a mile or more away, two big canoes bucked against the wind. They were coming up from Lac la Ronge, making for Nistowiak. Duncan tried his telescope. Each canoe held several men. North West Company? Hudson's Bay? He couldn't make them out. Not Indians, that was sure.

Should he signal them? Would they have news?... He turned to Cut Hand. The old man shook his head, then dowsed the fire. The canoes passed on.

Once above the rapids with the wind hard on their backs, they ran swiftly down towards Hunter Bay. The leaves were stripped now and the rocks looked grey and cold. In four hours they could see the familiar rocky point, a smudge of smoke. From somewhere came the loon's mournful, wind-torn cry. It came again and again. It drew a single faint reply. They'd soon be leaving now, the loons.

The point ahead stood up against the grey-white sky. Smoke blew through the jack pines. And it had changed. All changed. His post? Silent Partridge's teepee? There was nothing there. No palisade, no cabin.

They came closer, borne down by the wind. Not paddling now, silent and aghast. His post was gone. The trees where it had been were scorched and seared by fire.

Gulls rose in a screeching cloud from the rock as they drew near. There lay the remnants of a human form. Cut Hand growled to the women to keep the children in the canoes. Duncan went with him and they looked down at the slashed and mutilated form of Silent Partridge. His bloodied knife and broken musket lay nearby. He had died in agony. And the gulls' work too was well begun.

"Who has done this?" Cold anger was in Cut Hand's voice. His eyes swept the lake. Only grey waves and rocks and wind-blown sky.

Duncan followed him up the slope, dreading what they must now see. It was a waste of ash. Smoke was still plucked from it by the wind. They each took an unburned pole from the wreckage of the dead man's teepee. Charred logs

— some still glowing — the jumble of the broken palisade. Scorched rocks. They stepped through the carnage, feeling the heat still there, prodding with their poles.

This would have been the cabin door. They pulled aside burned posts, a heavy log. Cut Hand put his hand on Duncan's shoulder. Beneath another log was an all-but-cindered body.

They stooped and moved the smouldering log away. Welded to the breast of Laughing One was the tiny blackened bundle of her baby. She had held it to the last.

14
The Hunt

Only the boy still lived. They glimpsed his forlorn, half-naked little figure ghosting back between the pines. Rose Flower advanced to their edge and called and called in a gentle voice. At last he came out, step by fearful step. He curled up in her arms and quaked with the cold and the fear, and the devastation of his life.

Duncan and Cut Hand combed through the bush till they found a level place with sufficient soil. They dug a single grave, lined it with spruce. Among the ruins of the teepee were a few belongings. They buried them with the pitiful human remnants to help them on their journey. The women and the children cut back the brush to make a clearing. The orphaned boy, dream-like, pulled roots and cut shoots off with his knife.

Rose Flower and Snow Bird crouched with the children around the fire they built nearby. Their sorrowing chant went on and on, filling Duncan with matching sorrow and an agonized resolve. These were his people who had died. It was he who had brought their death. Just as surely as Ti'moine's. Just as surely as if he had pulled the trigger, fired the torch. Those two canoes had come for him.

He stood with Cut Hand on the headland as the night drew in, at the place where Silent Partridge had been killed. Wind moaned in his ears. Waves rolled down from northwards and broke ceaselessly on the rocks below. Random flakes of snow blew in their faces from a leaden sky.

"The boy says two canoes with the English mark came last nightfall. Two traders with some ten canoemen," the old man growled. "Silent Partridge sent the family to the house when they approached. But the boy turned back to be with his father. He saw him die and ran away. Then came the fire."

Duncan had built the cabin with a strong barred door, and shutters with loopholes for defence. The best attack would be to burn it, driving the defenders out.

Cut Hand read his thoughts. "She chose to die inside with her babe," his voice was tight and low, "rather than be violated by those brutes."

"It was those two canoes we saw then." Duncan pointed to the north. "Men from the Hudson's Bay. Revenge against me, for the burning at Ile-à-la-Crosse." His throat tightened and he could barely say the words. "I brought this on them. It was me."

"But you or your men killed none of them. Without reason they have killed our kin." Cut Hand bowed his head. The thin chanting of the

173

women was in their ears. At last his chin came up and he looked north through the gathering dark. "So three of them must die."

"I'll follow them."

"We'll follow together. And we must be quick. They have a long start and big canoes. Very soon the lakes will freeze. The women will take the children to our winter camp."

The two moved fast in Duncan's canoe, with Cut Hand in the stern. They paddled hard upwind through a gusty chilling night, and ran the rapids without pause. Cut Hand knew them backwards and he had the eyes of a lynx. They trotted down the portage past Nistowiak and were across at Dawson's post by dawn. Their hammering finally brought a surly response.

"What the hell. . .Cameron? At this hour? Canoes? Yes. Fergus Macdonald went up. . ."

"No. Any others?"

"Oh, yes. Two. Yesterday. Time?" He couldn't remember. "They headed down. Hudson's Bay markings. . ." He didn't ask them in.

On through Manitou Lake, its stretches broken by one sharp drop with heavy water sluicing down and two broad shelving rapids. There was no stopping. They chewed dry meat as they moved. The channel that curved down the right side of the Grand Rapid was deep and full. When they ran out at the bottom and into Trade Lake, the nagging northeast wind hit them with full force. It swept across the wild expanse. They had to win each foot with short sharp digs through white-capped waves. At last they struggled to the north side, tucked against the shore and slogged and slogged from one point to the next.

It was well past dark when they came to the North West Company's tidy, well-founded Fort de Traite just above the Frog Portage. They turned in to speak to old Lucien Cadieux, the Post Master and Angus Cameron's one-time guide.

"Bienvenue, M'sieu Cameron. The son of Crooked Nose is always welcome. And my old friend Cut Hand too."

"I appreciate your welcome, Monsieur Cadieux." Duncan came right to the point. "You must know of all the events at Ile-à-la-Crosse? That I'm expelled from the company?"

"Bien oui. The birds did sing. But the son of Angus Cameron and the grandson of Cut Hand cannot be so bad. Especially one I held on my own knee ten years ago. More maybe. Remember?" He smiled broadly and spread his hands. "Here, you must have hot food and drink. Non! The other way about. Rum first. The best Jamaica."

Twenty-four hours straight paddling was beginning to tell. Duncan and Cut Hand both declined the rum. The food brought by Cadieux's young wife was piping hot and rich and good.

Duncan had met Cadieux again last fall, after crossing Frog Portage from the south. He was a jovial, pot-bellied, grey-haired man with one leg and a pair of shrewdly friendly eyes — perhaps a quarter Cree. He had been Angus Cameron's guide and interpreter from long before Duncan's childhood trip to Montreal. Afterwards, he had lost his leg and his loyalty was rewarded with this lucrative post.

Most of the sons he had sired by successive wives found good positions too. Raised by their father's firm and steady hand, they were alert, reliable and skilled. His daughters found homes with well-placed men — Post Masters, interpreters, artisans. Two, in fact, were country wives of certain grands bourgeois.

The Frog Portage was a crossroads of the trade. You could go east to Hudson's Bay, south to the Saskatchewan River, Lake Winnipeg and beyond, or north and west forever. Add his widespread family net, and there was little news and gossip Lucien Cadieux didn't hear or wouldn't share.

Cut Hand would not speak of a family affair, so Duncan did. "Cadieux, Cut Hand's brother's grandson and his wife and child have been killed at Lac la Ronge. Murdered."

"Murdered! Sacrement! Who?. . ." Cadieux was up, his peg leg ringing on the floor.

"People from the Hudson's Bay, we think. And they burned my post. Have you seen canoes?"

"That post of theirs at Reindeer River." His eyes were blazing. "Me. . .Cadieux. I'll wipe it out. I'll. . ."

"Hold fast, Cadieux. Canoes. Have you seen any canoes?"

"Oui. M'sieu Macdonald with the brigade for Athabasca, two days back. Then two canoes today. They stopped this morning — going down.

One man came to speak to me."

"This morning!" Duncan saw Cut Hand's eyes narrow. "They must have stopped along the way."

"For drinking," gritted Cut Hand. "To celebrate their brave conquest."

"That's so. The man, he says they want to buy a keg of rum. I stood in the bastion with my gun and I said go to hell." Cadieux spat. "You know, I saw that man before, with Angus Cameron's brigade. When you came up last fall. He was the fiddler. . . ."

"Pinet? Not Coco Pinet?"

"His name?" Cadieux shrugged. "I only heard him play that time, while the rest unloaded the canoes to dry out the packs. He's very good — for fiddling."

It fitted. Pinet. The deserter, finding a berth with the other company. "The rest, Cadieux?"

"I don't know. The canoemen, very rough. Canadiens. Some Yankees maybe. Renegades. Not Orkneymen — except one who looks a clerk. But the one who gave the orders, he was English. True English. You know, a dandy with that way they talk. Shiny boots, not moccasins. It seemed no place for him."

English. Shiny boots. The fiddler. Duncan looked at Cut Hand, eyes intense. "They could have got to Lac la Ronge from the south, those two canoes? From the Saskatchewan?"

"There is a way. Through the lake you call Montreal and down the river by our summer camping place."

Then it could be him. Whistler. With Pinet, the deserter, and a rag-tag crew. His heart beat faster. It fitted. Those killings. Whistler. Revenge. The Wolverine. . . .

Cadieux said, "Only one canoe went down the Missinippe. The other crossed the Frog Portage to the south."

"And shiny boots? Which way?. . ."

Cadieux shook his head. "Too far, m'sieu. I can't tell."

"Then we separate, my grandson," Cut Hand said without a second thought. "You cross the Frog Portage. You know the way. I'll follow the Missinippe. Will One Leg give me a canoe?"

"Yes. And a good man to help in your hunting. And I go with M'sieu Cameron myself. Those damn English, they. . ."

Cut Hand held up his hand. "Stay here in peace, One Leg. This is for our own family. You have yours to care for. This is not a trader's war. It's a matter for me and my grandson."

"Then eat, and sleep a few hours." Cadieux turned to Duncan. "You remember beyond the portage, the swamp and narrow water? You'll go faster at first light with some rest."

Cadieux wakened them in the dark, gave them powder, shot, a pistol each, dry meat and a good canoe for Cut Hand. It was colder and the sky had cleared and the shore was edged with ice. A mile downstream at a low grassy stretch of shore was the top of the Frog Portage. They parted

178

there. They had no need to speak.

Duncan watched Cut Hand continue on down-stream, swallowed by the icy mist.

He crossed the short hard-frozen portage, cracked the ice and launched his canoe in an almost stagnant pond. The mist-hung swamp, dead trees like phantom sentinels, the twisting stream, dotted islands. It broadened into miles and miles of open lake. The sun came up. The remembered rhythm of the women's dirge drove his paddle on and on.

The wind increased. It was at his back but it was bitter cold. The sky above was clear, ice-blue. Waves built up and their crests broke white. Ice built on the gunwales. His coat was armoured hard with frozen spray. His hands were numbed. The wind would favour Whistler. They'd hoist a sail and fly like a storm-chased goose. Too dangerous in this small canoe.

A series of small lakes and narrows twisted through great grey rocky outcrops, topped with spruce and sheltered from the wind. Night drew in. The wind dropped with the sun but the cold deepened even more.

The channel narrowed and the water moved more quickly. There were three branches ahead. He remembered a sharp and sudden drop. With the wind down, he could hear its voice. The left chute looked as though it might be run, but it was too dark now for safety. He worked in to shore and ran across the portage in a single lift.

Then at the bottom his blood began to race. The spot had been used time and time again for stopping, but the rocks set for the fireplace were still warm. So were the ashes. They had not been dowsed. Someone had left here very recently. It could be Whistler. His neck began to crawl. It could, indeed, be Whistler. And not that far ahead.

The site was littered. A gum pot, birch bark, some cut-off strands of watape — the spruce root used for sewing bark — even a crooked knife. All the earmarks of a canoe damaged at the drop and brought in for repair. Perhaps they'd picked the wrong channel. As well, there was a shattered crock and the remnants of a keg.

'HBCoy' was stencilled on its broken end. He rolled it, and a half cup of liquor slopped out. So they'd been here for a time and they'd warmed themselves with rum. Then — slovenly crew that they were — they'd gone on, leaving important things behind, and a smouldering fire. This then was how he'd closed the gap. If Cadieux had sold them another keg of rum, they might still be here!

Icy points of stars reflected in the smooth water ahead. It was only a couple of miles to Medicine Rapid. They'd surely have gone past there — to Pelican Narrows at least. He raced on. Above, the vast green curtain of the northern lights leaped and writhed and glowed.

A half mile off he heard the rapid. At the same time he saw the black tuft of the lob-stick to guide him in. It was a high-growing pine with all but the top branches trimmed and it reared above the others, up against the weirdly lighted sky. Should he rest at the portage or go on? He was dog tired. In any event, he wouldn't risk the rapid in the dark.

Just below the lob-stick. . .what was that?

A prick of fire. A trail of rising sparks. He laid his paddle across the gunwales and watched. The canoe slid silently ahead. Imagination? No. More sparks rose, then a flare-up. A campfire. Someone throwing on a log.

The sound of water was louder now. The shore was slipping by. The lake narrowed quickly, funnelling towards the rapid. He whisked his paddle in short strokes, keeping it in the water, silent. The canoe slid sideways into shore.

There were bare overhanging alders here. He tucked in close. The portage was — which side? Yes. The left, and straight ahead. His mind raced. Fatigue was gone. His hunter's blood coursed fast.

The picture formed in his mind. Medicine Rapid to the right. One single, rock-cleft chute. Just at its top, five men, maybe more, under the upturned canoe. He could see its outline now, its bottom towards him, silhouetted by the fire. The canoemen would be warm and sheltered underneath. Where was the bourgeois? Whistler, or the other. He would have his tent. . . .

A little closer. Just ahead a beaver-felled poplar, half submerged. He gripped a branch. By the fire a figure moved. Sparks. Another log went on. It would be quite bright there. They wouldn't see behind the circle of the fire.

He looked along the shore. Another overhanging branch. He let himself drift down, reached up and caught it. It snapped. Dry, brittle. The sound was like a pistol, and it splashed.

Two quick draw strokes with his paddle and he was in to shore, heart thumping, watching, listening. They hadn't heard. Two men were hunched at the canoe. Repairing it, most likely. Their work a few miles back had not stood up. The fire flared a little and then died.

Yes. There beyond the canoe and past the fire stood the bourgeois' tent. A low white triangle at the foot of the big lob-pine. Firelight flickered on it and on the scaly redness of the bark.

Time passed. The repairs were finished. The two men turned in. He waited a full hour, watching the stars revolve, the shimmering of the lights above. A muskrat splashed. The only other sounds came from his own breathing and the rapid.

His mind was as clear and cold as the first black ice of winter. He was going to kill a man, two men. . . . First, the leader. If it was Whistler, well and good. He must strike like lightning and get out. Escape. If he crippled their canoe, he'd be well upstream before they could follow. He could hide in a hundred different inlets. If they chased him, he could ambush them, perhaps pick off another. . .

He took off his buckskin coat, retied his sash so the ends were tucked away and his sheath knife free. He reprimed his musket and pistol and pulled them both to full cock, tucked the pistol in his sash. He looked up once at the glorious spreading sky, took a deep breath of the icy air. Then he drifted towards the camp.

The sound of the rapid rose. The lob-pine reached high against the flaring sky. He slipped in where the great smooth slab of rock sloped down to meet the water. Silently he stepped ashore. There was a little ice right at the water's edge. He must be careful there. He placed his paddle on top of his pack in the canoe. Then he eased its bow out until it was at right angles to the shore. With one hand he lifted the stern and grounded it silently on the rock. That was his retreat.

He took his musket in one hand, the axe in the other. Doubled over, he crept up to the big canoe. Carefully he leaned the handle of the axe against its curve. He could see the fresh gum of the repair. It had been a major job. He knelt and listened.

Only feet away, underneath that shell of a canoe — how many men? He could hear their heavy breathing. His hand went to his knife. He eased it in its sheath, positioned it behind his hip.

Now. Slowly he straightened, musket ready. His eyes rose. Up. Up. Above the level of the canoe. He could see the tip of the tent now, beyond the fire. A little further. He could see its flap, the firelight on it. Then the fire itself. Nothing moved.

A log slumped and crackled. He froze. Sparks drifted up. A growl from beneath the canoe. Silence. . . .

He skirted the canoe, circled the fire. Bent double he ghosted in beside the tent. He held his breath, his left ear at the canvas. Sound of breathing. One, or two? He couldn't tell. He glanced at the fire, the canoe beyond it, gunwale up, blackness underneath. No movement there.

The tent flap was in his left hand, the musket in his right. He tugged. The tent shook. No change in the pace of the breathing inside. He tugged again. Harder. There was a grunt. Another tug. He heard a quizzical growl, then movement from inside.

"What's that?" The voice was half asleep.

He took a chance. "M'sieu. . ." he hissed. "Heh, m'sieu."

"Damnation. . ." A muttered curse. Then, "What the devil d'you want?" Whistler. Oh God, it was. His voice. Movement in the tent, some muffled words.

"Ici, m'sieu," Duncan wheezed. "S'vous plaît. . ."

The canvas bulged. He levelled his musket. His stomach churned.

The flap moved. Only feet away. One squeeze of the trigger to blow that head right off. Hair black. Touched by firelight, glowing copper. This was wrong. Face in darkness still, turning towards him. He'd. . .

No. . .no. . .no! The words ripped silent from his throat. He saw the face. Her face. Looking dead at him with her level open gaze.

It was Nancy Spence.

15
Medicine Rapid

"No!" He stood, recoiled. The world lurched.

"Nancy. Nancy. . ." His chest filled, his throat jammed tight. He stood immobile, looking down. What was this? What was she doing? What had she done?

She gasped, her eyes wide. Shame? Fear? Love? Hate? He couldn't see her face. Her eyes said?. . . He couldn't tell.

Nancy. . .Whistler.

"What the bloody hell?" Whistler's voice behind her in the tent. Loud. Angry. Duncan just looked at her. How long?. . . How long?

A sudden flick of Nancy's head. She looked past Duncan's shoulder, mouth wide, breath drawn in.

He spun about. A dark figure rushed at him. A knife glistened. He brought his musket half up, fired. The man stopped dead, folded forward.

Whistler next. Duncan felt cold, steady, unhurried. Time stopped. He dropped his empty musket, drew his knife, tugged his pistol free.

Shouts. More movement by the fire. The camp was up in arms.

He faced the tent, Nancy crouching by it. Behind her. . .Whistler. He saw him now. Just his head. One arm held her back against his chest. A pistol in his other hand right by her head. Duncan raised his own. There was fear in Whistler's eyes.

But no target. Only Nancy, shielding Whistler. If he turned away, he would be shot. If he attacked? Nancy. Nancy.

Noise behind. He whirled. Men blundering at him through the dark. He fired at the first of them, leaped aside, heard a roar of rage. Then a pistol shot behind him. Whistler. He didn't turn. He went straight for the fire and hurdled it, vaulted the canoe, dropped in its shadow. His axe. Right there. He gripped it, swung it high and brought it down.

It ripped right through the skin of the canoe. Bark flew. He tugged. It jammed. A shout. He wrenched it clear. He raised it, swung again. Wood splintered. Once more. Shouts, close by now. A huge hole opened.

He left the axe, turned, looked straight at a musket barrel. Straight at its cold black eye. Instinctively his hand came up to knock it and he ducked. In the instant of its flash he saw a face tucked to the butt. A face. . . Duncan's cheek was seared. He heard the thunder in his ear.

The blaze half blinded him. He lurched forward, stumbled for his canoe, lifted, launched and tumbled in. He fumbled for his paddle, still dazzled, trying to clear the gunflash from his eyes. He was afloat, but going where?

He could hear the rapid. It would draw him over. . .away from them, at least. More shouts ashore, then two quick musket shots. His eyes were clearing somewhat now.

There. He had his paddle. He could vaguely make things out — the fire ashore, figures moving. His canoe was swinging in the current. The sound of the rapid was louder now, and louder. He was broadside to the stream and moving fast.

He reached out with his paddle and spun the canoe. He was in the current's grip. No turning back now. Dark figures ran along the rock. Musket flashes. Thunder. Balls whacked the water and cracked through the canoe. Another buzzed right by his head.

There was the gateway to the rapid now. A smooth slick. Black, reflecting stars with raging white below. Rollers curled from either shore, angling down towards the middle. A great V, its point downstream, was there to draw him in — to funnel him amongst those giant waves. He reached back with his paddle, pulled his stern across the current, away from the guns. He dug in hard and pulled. Again, again, again. He crabbed towards the right-hand shore.

Another fusillade tore up the water. Then he heard a whack and felt a monstrous blow. It knocked his knee from under him, and he pitched into the bottom of the canoe.

Hit. No doubt. But he felt nothing. He struggled up and sat. He could still reach behind and to the right with his paddle, drawing the canoe closer to shore and the start of those big white waves. Flashes. Perhaps they fired again. He could hear nothing but the roar of water.

He held his canoe back against the current, pulled it over, over. Then he felt the downwards tilting of the water, switched his paddle, drove the bow hard right, then braced. Straight into the wave it went. It lifted beautifully, bucked like a wild horse once, twice, three times. He straightened up. Water showered. He passed the towering stack of raging white.

The water ceased to shout. The thunder of the chute dropped behind. The canoe drifted, rolling sluggishly. Water slopped, ice-cold. He would have to get ashore and empty out. Behind, the bottom of the chute boiled luminously white. Above that, the rocky cleft. Then the tree tops, the lob-stick, those curling banners in the northern sky.

Water in the canoe. Very cold. Getting deeper too. Bullet holes. That's right. They'd hit it. Hit him too, hadn't they?. . . Leg. Thigh. It must be bleeding, but he felt nothing. Nothing. He could go safely to the right-hand bank, empty the canoe, perhaps plug up the holes. They'd not follow for a while with their smashed canoe. They couldn't catch him now. Difficult to paddle, though. That leg. . .

Curious. The face behind the musket. . .the one who'd nearly shot him, half blinded him. It was Pinet. No doubt of that. Coco Pinet.

But did it matter? His head dropped on his chest. Did it really matter? The dark. The firelight and the tent. And Nancy Spence. Nancy Spence with Whistler. Nancy Spence. . .

And he had failed. One. . .two men shot perhaps. But he'd missed his chance at Whistler. He could have killed him in his tent. If he'd only acted. He could have yanked that Nancy Spence aside, plunged in and shot him where he lay. Instead, he'd pulled back, wavered. Failed.

Failed Silent Partridge and his wife and child. Failed Cut Hand. All the family. He'd failed Quick Feet too. All those the Wolverine had killed. He had failed them all. His lack of stomach, his weakness. . . And Nancy Spence was Whistler's woman.

No, it didn't matter if he never reached the shore. . .didn't empty the canoe, bind his wound, build a fire before he froze. . . Nothing mattered. Nothing mattered now. . . .

Nothing.

16
Winter

A Cree called Ragged Man found Duncan on the island where he kept his dogs. They were slinking around a battered canoe and the form of a young man — so near death that it was just a matter of time before the starved wretches tore his body apart. They had already robbed the canoe and ripped off half his clothes.

Ragged Man and his wife rifled his remaining possessions and almost left him to die. At the last minute, though, they decided to try to revive him in hope of some reward. How he had got there from Medicine Rapid Duncan never knew. Later he had only the vaguest remembrance of being moved, and had no idea when it was that Cut Hand came.

The old man was there beside him when he first awoke. He tended the fire in the middle of the teepee and renewed the infusion of balsam that steamed away in the kettle. Duncan's lungs were full of liquid. He coughed in wracking bouts. His face was ravaged, his cheeks sunken.

His eyes were deep black holes. But the balsam brought relief. Another medicine eased his fever. Warm poultices reduced the agony of the shattered leg.

"The canoe I followed stopped at the Deer River," Cut Hand said. "The English from the Bay have a small post there. I begged some tobacco and powder from the trader." He put on a whining tone and stretched out his hands. "For a poor man — a poor man who has lost all his goods. But I will bring skins at the turn of the year. . . . He gave me credit so I wouldn't go to the post across the river. No Englishman was with that canoe, Grandson. Only a rabble of Canadian canoemen, waiting for a packet to take to the sea."

"So you turned back and followed me, Grandfather. But it's winter now. . . ." It was difficult to keep things straight.

"Winter was close when I passed the Frog Portage, so I sent word by One Leg's man to The Otter to follow me with dogs as soon as he could. I came by canoe, like you. The ice is strong enough to travel now. He'll be here soon."

The agony of his leg, the wearying cough, the bouts of feverish sweating and trembling gradually grew less. At last he had the strength to sit and the stomach to watch as Cut Hand unwound the bandage from his leg. The ball had ripped through the flesh and muscle of his thigh, broken the bone and glanced off. Cut Hand had closed the wound skilfully with sinews. His poultices had cleansed it too and drawn the pain.

The whole nightmare of Medicine Rapid shadowed Duncan's mind. What he could have done, what he should have done, what he failed to do. . . . Nancy Spence's face dogged him through it all, haunting the half delirium of his dreams. As his pain and sickness lessened, the torment of those past events grew and grew.

He woke one night to the sound of wolves. Cut Hand was sitting across the fire watching him. Deep lines were carved between his eyes.

He said, "Your body's mending, Grandson, but your mind is troubled."

Duncan looked into the fire, hollow eyed, his face still gaunt. Cut Hand had scarcely left his side for. . .how long? And never in all that time had he asked one single question.

"There was a fight, Grandfather, at Medicine Rapid. One, perhaps two, died. But not the Wolverine."

He avoided the other's eyes, looked up at the thinly rising smoke. "I failed. I could have killed him, but I failed."

Cut Hand nodded slightly. He put a stick on the fire. There was silence in the teepee. Outside the wolves began again.

Then suddenly, "Grandfather, I must tell you. . ." and it all came pouring out. Like a river when it breaks in spring. Every word. . .just as it had happened, just as it had gone through his mind so many times. And each word built on the agony of the last. His attraction to Nancy

Spence. Whistler. The murder on the ice at Watchusk Bay. His own treachery at Ile-à-la-Crosse, and Ti'moine's death. Disgrace. Exile by his own father, and still his futile yearning after Nancy Spence. Finally at Medicine Rapid, with the Wolverine's life right in his hands. . . .

"I could have, Grandfather." His own words stabbed him to the bone. "I could have just brushed her aside and killed him. But I failed."

It was all there, shameful, ugly and a vast relief, like the lancing of a festered wound. But he could not ask forgiveness. He had earned nothing but contempt.

Silently Cut Hand took a small braid of sweet grass from his medicine bag. He put it on the glowing coals and it burned with a bright clear flame. It filled the teepee with its scent. Then he said, "Show me a man who has done nothing of which he is ashamed. Tell me who has never wandered from the path. Finding it again, you find yourself. You find the truth."

Their eyes met across the flame.

"The Wolverine will die for his crimes," Cut Hand said quietly, "and you'll see to it. As for the young woman, who can judge? You can only search your heart. If she's worthy, she is no doubt searching hers."

The sadness had gone from Cut Hand's eyes. Duncan understood then that everything he had said, in some way the old man already knew.

* * *

Of the long trip riding in the carriole to Cut Hand's winter camp, Duncan remembered only its end. The long flat layer of smoke hanging at tree-top level, motionless in the crystal air. The dogs scenting the camp and running full out across the last three miles of sparkling lake. The answering barking of the camp dogs. Then they were running in among the four teepees snugged among the trees and banked with snow.

The children rushed to meet them and piled on the toboggan, Raymond and Cat shouting, laughing, throwing their arms around him and their grandfather and The Otter. There were other children too, other people of the family. And there was Sally, then his mother, Rose Flower, helping old Snow Bird out to join the welcoming crowd.

The family closed around him and made him one of them. Rose Flower, with Sally as her shadow, nursed him. They cooked the choice cuts the hunters brought — the tongues and hearts and livers — and watched him grow in strength. And they talked — of family events, of things past, the children who had died that he had never seen, of Montreal and his life there. Gradually that ten-year void was filled.

His beard had grown. "Like a regular white man's," Sally said with some surprise. It was rather sparse, but a silky black and getting long. He shaved himself, to all the children's merriment, using a finely honed knife and Rose Flower's mirror.

His face had regained its healthy colour. The sunken cheeks had filled in somewhat, but the line of his jaw was sharper and his cheekbones were more clearly chiselled. The bridge of his nose seemed higher and his dark-brown eyes more deeply set. His wide mouth opened, though, in laughter. His strength rebuilt.

As winter drew towards spring, he sat in the warming sun with the books that had come up-river from Angus Cameron in the fall. He and Sally read to Raymond and Cat. Malcolm, nearly two, sat on his good knee. Others of all ages joined them. If they couldn't understand the English, they enjoyed the music of the words.

He reread the instruction Angus Cameron had written inside the volume of Burns' poems. Here and there a word in the lines on page 29 had been changed in pencil, perhaps to make more sense in this wildly different land. He picked a time when he and his mother were sitting in the sunshine alone, and he read:

> O, my luve's like the red, red rose,
> That's newly sprung in June:
> O, my luve's like the melodie
> That's sweetly played in tune.
>
> As fair thou art, my bonnie lass,
> So deep in luve am I;
> And I will luve thee still, my dear,
> Till a' the lakes go dry.

Till a' the lakes go dry, my dear,
And the rocks melt wi' the sun:
I will luve thee still, my dear,
While the sands o' life shall run.

And fare thee well, my only luve!
And fare thee well a while!
And I will come again, my luve,
Though it were ten thousand mile.

Her lined face softened as he read and the sun seemed to shine more warmly than before. She put her hand on his and thanked him. Yes, she believed it. She believed her husband would come again. But Duncan's mind was gnawed with doubt.

Sally spotted the inscription in one of the books that had come from Marianne.

"An 'X' means a kiss, Duncan, doesn't it?" She was sitting on the soft skins in the teepee with the book in her lap. Her legs were crossed, skirt stretched across her knees, with a hand holding each moccasined toe. Teasing? Duncan looked at her. No. Her face was still and her eyes were serious.

"Why, yes. In a way," he said carefully. "It's . . .between friends."

"You used to write letters telling all about the Letelliers and Marianne." She paused, then took a breath and looked up at him. Her face was set.

"Did you ever kiss her, Duncan?"

"Well, I. . .yes."

"Do you love her then?"

"Oh, come on, Weasel."

"And Nancy. What about her?"

"I. . .look, Weasel, it's not your business."

"But you love Nancy, don't you? Those messages I took. And you've been waiting all this time for word from her. I know. Aren't you going to marry her someday?"

"Forget about it, Sally, please," he said flatly, looking deliberately down at his book. Till now he had simply told her that he had been wounded in a fight with Whistler's men. He hadn't mentioned Nancy to anyone — including their mother — and Cut Hand, of course, wouldn't tell a soul.

"Forget?" Sally wouldn't be deflected. "I like Nancy, Duncan. You. . .you can't just. . .forget."

He bit his lip.

"Well, can you?"

"No, you're right." He found his voice. "But things change, Weasel."

"People don't. That's what Grandfather says." Her voice was defiant, her eyes intent. "It's what Mother says about Father."

As gently as he could, Duncan said, "Nancy is Whistler's wife now. She was with him at Medicine Rapid. Some people do change, Sally. Or. . . maybe we just don't see them properly in the first place."

"Whistler's wife." Sally breathed the words.

197

"Whistler's wife." A long silence except for distant children's laughter and the barking of a dog.

"Well then..." Her lip was trembling. "Will you go back to Marianne?"

To make his fortune and go back to Marianne and Montreal. He looked at the new leggings, fringed shirt and winter moccasins that Grandmother and Rose Flower had made him. And his beaded glengarry hanging on one of the teepee's poles.

"Maybe we're just too far apart," he said.

"Too far apart. . . ." There were tears in Sally's eyes.

Young Raymond came back with Cut Hand from his trapline. "I set the trap myself. Grandfather showed me where and he helped with some magic. It caught the marten. And I skinned it too and stretched it. Look!" His face was alive with excitement. He ran his hand over the glossy fur and held it out for Duncan.

"What will you give me in trade?" Raymond laughed, almost bursting with happiness. "No. It's for Grandmother. I'll catch enough to make her a beautiful coat."

"He'll make a good hunter." Cut Hand smiled with pride. "He listens and he watches. He learns and understands."

The alert, active little face, with the teeth too large, was firming up, taking on character. Even the Cameron nose was beginning to show.

Later when they were alone, Cut Hand said, "His father might allow him to stay with me and your mother and the young ones this summer too."

"I'm afraid Father wants him to go to Montreal with Sally," Duncan said, "to learn from others." He wished he had known how to say it better. His awkwardness with Cree made it sound rude and thankless. But Raymond was growing as an Indian boy already. What a harsh jolt that school was going to be. As for Sally, another year or two in the northwest and she'd be the country bride of a Balfour or a Benson or Maclaren. Far better she should be in school.

"I'll take them to Fort William myself in the spring, Grandfather." He didn't want to send them with Maclaren, but he only said, "There may be troubles on the way."

With them safe in their father's hands, he could get on the trail of the Wolverine. He had no idea where that might lead.

Spring came at last with that tinkling rush, that silent deep-drawn sigh that says life has come back to the earth. Mist hung above the lake, softly tinted by the sun. Ice receded from the shore and shifted with the wind.

Geese clamoured through in giant flights and rested by the open water. They'd sleep, heads under wings, with one sentinel to watch, his neck stretched full. Then at some signal they would lift off shouting towards their nesting grounds.

Mosquitoes swarmed, feed for the darting swallows which nested in the bank nearby. Smudge fires clouded the camp with smoke. The boys shot jack-fish in the creeks with their bows and arrows. They roasted some on sticks themselves and fed others to the dogs. Belle produced a litter of nine fine pups. Trusting, she licked Duncan's hand as he picked them up in turn. Each had the touch of wolf and the unmistakable cast of old Gran' Bleu.

Duncan gave them, with their mother, to the orphaned son of Silent Partridge. The boy tumbled with the pups in sheer delight. The Otter and his wife had adopted the little fellow as their own, and Duncan gave the rest of his dogs to them.

Days of slanting rain, wet feet and sodden clothes, and the grey-pocked ice was gone. The canoes were gummed, the winter's furs and household goods were bundled, the skins were taken from the teepees and the poles left standing. It was time to leave the winter camp.

Rose Flower stood with Duncan by the canoes. "These months have been my greatest happiness, Duncan," she said. "At Ile-à-la-Crosse, when you first came home, we could scarcely talk. I wondered if you were still my son. Then I lost you again. Then once again. And now?"

When he had seen her on the landing that first

day, Duncan had sensed her strength. Now he had found his way past the gaunt lines and colour of her face and her scant command of English, and beyond the gulf that had been opened by the years. He knew her tenderness and wisdom and the depth of love she had for all her family. At this moment he could feel it and he could see it in her eyes.

"We can never lose each other, Mother," he said. "Not now."

Life and strength had come back to Duncan Cameron. It was time to leave his family. But now he had no wish to go.

17
Fort William

It was a cheerless, rain-lashed day when they reached the place for the summer camp. It was deserted except for the skeletons of last year's teepees. Duncan, Sally and Raymond said goodbye to their mother there, and to Cat and lively little Malcolm, and Snow Bird and all their family. Then Cut Hand and The Otter took them down to the Rapid River post.

They traded their furs with Dawson, then camped on the Nistowiak side of the river. Feelings would still run against Duncan at Ile-à-la-Crosse; so when the brigade came through, he sent a letter to Peter Maclaren via Cut Hand. The three Camerons would go down later with Fergus Macdonald and the Athabasca brigade.

For Macdonald's arrival, Cut Hand dressed in the crimson splendour of his captain's coat, emblazoned with silver. "Gifts given and gifts received. These are the mark of a man," he said to Duncan. "The important things are neither bought nor sold."

The coat had been given to him by the great Alexander Mackenzie twenty years before, as had the big silver medal with the likeness of the king. The glittering gorget at his throat and the pierced silver band around his tall beaver — and the hat itself — had been among the gifts of Crooked Nose when Cut Hand had given him Rose Flower as his bride. For the first time, he had on the dirk which Duncan had brought him, and he wore it with equal pride.

There was no fur trading to be done with Macdonald. Dressing in his regalia was a matter of showing due respect to the Red Haired One Who Laughs, as Cut Hand always called him. Also he had a favour to ask.

"Red Hair values loyalty above all things," he said to Duncan. "But he has little compassion. It's best that I ask your passage for you."

The brigade swept in at midday, and Macdonald greeted the old man warmly.

"Cut Hand, my friend of many years! Come and smoke the calumet." His glance rested for one cold second on the lean young half-breed in deerskin and beaded cap who waited in the stern of the canoe.

The two walked slowly to the post, followed by Dawson, Balfour and a somewhat trimmer Wee Willie MacGillivray. They too ignored him. The canoemen showed their usual brief jay-like curiosity in what was going on between the great men. Then they went back to their pipes and chatter and horseplay and profane jokes.

In an hour Macdonald walked down to the water. "For my friend Cut Hand," he said to Duncan brusquely, "I have agreed to give passage to you as well as Angus Cameron's children. In wi' ye."

When they stopped that night and the canoes were unloaded and the cooking fires set, Duncan went to Fergus Macdonald. He found him enjoying a dram with Balfour and MacGillivray, while a handsome young Chipewyan woman pitched his tent.

"Mr. Macdonald, I'm not welcome at the gentlemen's fire. That I know. I rode in the canoe today with my brother and sister because of Cut Hand. You gave the favour of my passage to him, not me. I have my own paddle. I'll work my way."

Macdonald looked hard at him, his lips pressed tight. Balfour and MacGillivray studied their feet.

"Bonhomme!" Macdonald shouted. He didn't take his eyes from Duncan's. The brigade guide came over. "Bonhomme, Cameron here is an engagé now. Common canoeman. He can join the milieux. Pay him off at Fort William."

It was early August when they carried down the Mountain Portage past the mighty drop of Kakabeka Falls. Duncan trotted quickly with his two ninety-pound fur packs, then ran back up for his second load. Moccasins, a breech clout, a scrap of shirt and a sweatband around his head.

He was mahogany brown, rawhide tough from the months of paddling and packing, and his limp had all but gone.

Sally literally danced down the path with her pack. Raymond chattered endlessly behind her. The white-throated sparrows sang through the broiling midday heat. The voice of the great waterfall urged them on.

The voyageurs whooped and shouted. In the great back eddy at the bottom of the falls they bathed and shaved and changed into their clean shirts and their finery and feathers. For them the bawdy pleasures of Fort William lay just ahead. For Sally and Raymond this was the joyous day they'd see their father. For Duncan it was uncertainty about so many things.

The only possible trace of Whistler he had found was a report at Bas de la Rivière. An Englishman with one canoe had come down Lake Winnipeg very early, and gone up the Red River, heading south. That was two months back. . . .

Now came the roofs, palisades and bastions of Fort William. The vast open sea of Lake Superior stretched out beyond. The sound of pipes reached out to welcome them. Cannon boomed. Fergus Macdonald stood in the lead canoe, waving his beaver, his white hair streaming. The brigade swept in with the precision of a naval squadron. Muskets crashed a welcome volley. Raymond gasped and Sally clapped for joy. This was far grander, far more splendid than Ile-à-la-Crosse.

They came alongside the log-cribbed landing to waves and shouts and cheers.

Duncan looked up at the crowds and a cluster of tall-hatted gentlemen in their latest fashions. Tail coats, ruffled shirts, gleaming boots, silver-knobbed canes. MacGillivray, Beaupré, Fraser, Macdonnell, MacTavish, Letellier. Yes, there was Raymond Letellier. All up from Montreal. Some wintering partners were here too, looking somewhat more roughshod. But Angus Cameron?

"Come on, Duncan, let's find Father." Sally tugged at his sleeve.

"Up you get then, both of you. I've got to stay and unload. I'm a canoeman, remember." They dashed off.

Fergus Macdonald was there now, shaking hands and slapping backs. Old MacGillivray was greeting nephew Wee Willie as though he'd been gone ten years. . . . But no Angus Cameron.

A crowd of pork-eaters — voyageurs from Montreal — shouted cheerful insults. Indian and half-breed girls waved and smiled. Exchanges in French, Ojibway, Cree. Children gathered, peered wide-eyed at the fabled newcomers. The pipes skirled on.

"Duncan. Father's not here." Raymond was kneeling on the landing, his eyes huge. "He's not here. And he said. . .he promised. . ." Sally was behind him now, her lip trembling.

"Don't worry, we'll find him. Look, Sally, the gentleman in the green coat and red waistcoat. See? It's Monsieur Letellier. Go see him and take

Raymond. Tell him who you are. I'll be along. . ."

"Déchargez les canots, mes petits. Déchargez."
Bonhomme's order to unload cut through the
cheerful noise.

Raymond Letellier stood with his back to Duncan, looking out the dormer of his private room.
His tail coat hung over the chair, and his shirt
collar was open in the heat of the late afternoon.
He'd seemed genuinely glad to see the young
man who had been his ward for so many years —
in spite of his disgrace and his canoeman's dress.
They spoke in French, as they always had in
Montreal.

The familiar aquiline face had aged a little,
and there were touches of grey in his thick black
hair. But his body was still lean as whipcord, and
he had that glow of good health on his swarthy
cheeks — as though he'd just been on his early-
morning ride.

"The man Whistler, sir. Has there been any
news?"

Letellier shook his head. "The warrant your
father wrote at Ile-à-la-Crosse went everywhere
— including the Hudson's Bay governor and all
their factories. I hardly think they'd pay much
attention to one dead Indian, though. Particularly
with the companies almost in a state of war.
They might be more inclined to give him a
reward."

"Well, he has killed again. A man, woman and

child. At Lac la Ronge." A bitter taste rose in Duncan's mouth. "Three more — dead Indians, as you call them, sir. They happen to be my cousins."

"Your cousins?" Letellier looked sharply at him. "You can swear out another warrant. If he shows up at any of our posts, of course. . ."

"Which he's hardly likely to do," Duncan said half to himself. "So it's up to me."

"Duncan. . ." Letellier took a breath and turned half away again. "I didn't tell Sally and Raymond, but I think your father may not go back up to le pays d'en haut."

"Is he still ill then? Isn't he better?"

"I had a letter, written in March. The Edinburgh surgeons were successful. They removed the stones and he recovered well." Letellier paused and pursed his lips. Then he went on quickly. "Well enough, from what he said, to get married."

"Married? What d'you mean. . .married?"

"An Edinburgh lady, it seems."

"An Edinburgh lady!" Duncan went cold. He heard the echo of his own voice. "An Edinburgh lady." It had happened then. It had happened.

"He. . .he couldn't. He couldn't do it."

"I know what you're thinking, Duncan. It's hard for you. But it's not. . .unusual. He'll look after everything, your mother. . ."

"She's his wife. My mother's his wife." Duncan could barely hear himself. "She's not just to be. . .looked after."

"Duncan, don't judge too quickly." Letellier

put up his hand. "Misunderstandings. Letters can go astray. He may be far sicker than we think. Too ill to go back to the northwest. Any number of things."

That Christmas, he'd said, 'To my Bonnie. And may every one of us live long in happiness together. . . .' Last fall, that letter and the book, the poem. 'And I will come again, my luve, though it were ten thousand mile.'

A poet's words. His own father's words. But they were only words. So he was no different from the rest. From all the other white men. Words were one thing, deeds another.

She had fed him, stitched his clothes, made his moccasins, webbed his snowshoes, nursed him when he was sick, borne and raised his children. She had taught him to speak the language. She had linked him with her people, made him a great trader. She had travelled with him thousands of miles. Summer, winter. Lit his fires and cooked and kept him warm. She had made a home for him, place after place in the farthest corners of her own harsh land. And, above all, she had loved him.

She had loved him and he had turned her off. Turned her off in favour of some elegant lady in a civilized city who could no more do the things that Rose Flower did for Angus Cameron — day after day for twenty years — than she could swim across the ocean.

"Is he. . .coming back to Montreal?" Anger rose in Duncan's throat.

Letellier saw his outrage. He kept his words as even as he could. "I expect so, Duncan. To tidy his affairs. He's a rich man, you know, and he wants to retire. If I were in his shoes, I'd buy a nice estate near Montreal and enjoy the fruits of my labours." He raised his eyebrows. "But I'm a Canadian, not a Scot. He might go back. They all say their hearts are in the Highlands."

"What about Sally and Raymond?" He struggled for control.

"The schools are arranged and paid for, and they'll stay with us in the holidays, as you did. He sent a bank draft for you too, for five hundred pounds."

"What for?"

Letellier shrugged. "Perhaps it was in case he didn't fare well in Edinburgh."

"Or fared too well," Duncan said bitterly. "So he paid me off. In advance. As he's going to pay off my mother. What kind of man is he?" His voice rose. "My own father. What kind of man?. . ."

"Duncan," Letellier flung back, "just hold on. You can't judge your father's actions. And you should be damned well grateful for the money. You're in no position at all regarding the fur trade, you know. Your licence is up for review in the next couple of days."

Duncan swallowed hard. He said stiffly, "I must thank you for helping me last year, sir."

"Well, perhaps we'll find enough friends to swing the vote again," Letellier said a little curtly. "I'll try."

Duncan stalked through the lengthening shadows, not seeing the crowds swarming in the square, not hearing the laughter and shouts and music and song. The children must not know. Not yet. Their father must explain it all to them in Montreal. . .if and when he came. Or when he wrote. It would stab Sally to the heart. He knew that. And Raymond, even at his age. . . No. He must take them down to Montreal himself. The Wolverine would have to wait. Those two must not be alone when they found out. They must never be, as he was, all alone.

He found them by the gate.

"Where is he, Duncan? Where's Father? No one will tell us."

He led them to the riverside. It was deserted now, and quiet.

"Did you ever see a canoe as big as that?" Raymond was breathless. "And that huge house made of stone? And I saw. . ."

"I know, Raymond, there's so much to see. But listen to me, then you can show me everything." He tugged the little fellow down beside him. Sally was already sitting, hugging her knees. Her chin rested on them and her eyes followed the swallows dipping, darting.

Duncan put his arm around her shoulder. "He was very sick, you know. They had to cut out those stones. But he's fine now. Mr. Letellier told me."

"With a knife?" Raymond's eyes were wide. "Did they sew him up after?"

"I've been so afraid," Sally said.

"He'll be all right, Sally. You'll see him soon in Montreal."

The summer evening deepened. Nighthawks thrummed. Shouts and random singing grew. From the palisade a bugle sounded. At the main gate orders rang out for the evening gun.

"Load. . . Ready. . . Fire!" A single cannon boomed. The two young ones flinched beside him and he held them tight.

The smell of smoke hung in the still night air. Bullfrogs, snatches of song, a distant fiddle, the whippoorwill, all mingled with the murmur of the river.

An Edinburgh lady. He'd married an Edinburgh lady.

He kept his voice steady. "I'll go with you down to Montreal."

"Thank you, Duncan, thank you," Sally whispered, "but I'm still afraid."

From far off came the sound of pipes. Measured, slow and deeply sad. Someone, somewhere, was playing a lament.

18
Montreal

Going down with Letellier's brigade, Duncan
travelled as a gentleman. He shared the deep-
bellied comfort of a six-fathom canoe with the
young ones. To Sally and Raymond the final
day's run to Lachine was as exciting as the
breathless plunge down a high running rapid.
It took them into a whole new world.

The great canoes swept past golden fields,
strong stone houses and a blaze of scarlet maples.
Children raced along the shore with dogs barking
at their heels, cheering "les voyageurs." Now
ahead they saw the glint of the church spire at
Lachine and the sprawl of grey stone warehouses.
Duncan could see the crowds waiting to welcome
them. Then with the last lines of the canoemen's
paddling song, he spotted Marianne.

She was there among the forest of parasols
and the swirl of finely dressed ladies and gentlemen. He recognized her slender figure, her liveliness, her black hair and darting hands. He
watched as she flung her arms around her father,

213

spoke to him rapidly, then spun to look straight at the three Camerons in their canoe.

He saw her run towards them, skirts flying, her red lips parted in a smile. He remembered her bright cheeks and dancing eyes. He remembered too her closeness and the touch of her lips in that same stone warehouse right behind her. Two long years ago. He felt a sudden pang.

She laughed down at him. "Welcome, Duncan Cameron. And your sister and your brother. Welcome home." She knelt on the landing's edge and reached down and took his hand. She held it for a long moment and he felt her warmth and looked into those laughing eyes.

Angus Cameron wasn't in Montreal or he'd have come to Lachine to meet them. There must be mail at the company's city chambers, though, so Duncan ordered their calêche to rue Vincent.

Sally and Raymond were enthralled. There was the long and lovely drive past autumn fields and farms and windmills. Then finally the city, and everything was new. The cobbled streets, stone houses jammed in side by side, steepled churches, bright tin roofs, the masts and yards of ships. And strange stenches — breweries, tanneries, the slaughterhouse, the sewers and the street-side slops.

"And thousands and thousands of people," Sally gasped. And horses, and dogs and cats, and gulls and pigeons. . . .

Duncan had to shout while pointing out the sights because Raymond kept his hands clamped firmly over his ears. The clatter of wheels and hooves on cobbles, the shouts of teamsters, draymen, porters, hawkers. The clanging of church bells at their midday chorus. The bellowing of stevedores along the wharves. The bustle and hum of a whole city at its busiest time of year — all of it was just too much for a small boy from the Indian country.

Duncan took them into the familiar offices of Cameron, Letellier & Co.

"Young Mr. Cameron. . .it can't be. . . Why, it is. . ." Portly old Garneau, blinking delightedly over his half-moon spectacles, came down from the stool he had used for fifty years. "And these young people — I can see it. Monsieur Angus, he's written on their faces. What a pleasure. What a pleasure. . . ."

There was a letter. Yes, there was. It was bare of detail, but it was enough for the two children. Their father would soon be in Montreal. He had had a setback, but he was much better now and nearly ready to travel. Their spirits rose even higher. They rattled through the narrow streets and up the sunny reaches of the mountain. In through a pair of big stone gates they swung, wheels crunching on the gravel drive beneath the scarlet trees. They swept up to the front steps and wide verandah of the Letelliers' lovely house, the place where Duncan's boyhood years had come — and gone.

* * *

A crisp clear night and a stream of carriages rolled up to the door. Montreal society arrived in all its splendour to pay homage to the riches of the fur trade. The great house was filled with light and life and laughter.

Bubbling over and bejewelled, Tante Angèle received her guests. She admired Duncan's newly tailored evening clothes, kissed his lean brown cheek. He was so much darker now, from sun and wind and snow, so much more muscular and lithe. So much a man. She mock-scolded him for wearing his hair so long.

In the shadowed upper hall, Duncan found Sally and Raymond clinging to the banisters, peering in wonder at the marvellous scene below.

"Like Hogmanay, in the Great Hall." Raymond's eyes were huge. "Only. . .only. . ." He ran out of words.

The candles in the great chandelier cast their soft light on the bare shoulders of ladies and struck magic glitters from their jewels. The scarlet uniforms of the officers, the white shirts of gentlemen in evening dress, the gleam of silver and crystal and polished floors. Through the wide arch of the salon the dancers swirled and dipped. Music and voices and laughter blended with the gorgeous sight and climbed the stairs to wrap them in enchantment.

Sally looked up at Duncan. "Are all the houses in Montreal like this?" she breathed. "Do they always dance at night? It's. . .so beautiful."

"No, Sally, it's not always like this." He knelt

beside his sister and brother. "When you come to stay during the holidays, though, there'll be a great dance, and sleigh rides in winter, and picnics in summer. . ."

"And my room. It's my own with a huge feather bed. And look at this dress." She stepped away and spun around and the skirts flared out. It was dusty pink with a wide, darker pink sash. "And the slippers. And look what Tante Angèle gave me to wear with it." A string of tiny pearls gleamed against the darkness of her throat.

"Lovely lady," Duncan laughed, "come down and have a dance with me."

"Oh, I will. A little later." She looked down, suddenly shy. "But you should dance with Marianne. Look. There she is. She's beautiful, Duncan. And look at her dress. It's cut so low — like all the ladies."

"She's with that man in the red coat." Raymond pointed. "It's like Grandfather Cut Hand's, but it's not half as long and he hasn't got a medal."

"Go dance with her, Duncan." Sally pushed him. "She likes you. She told me it was wonderful to see you again, and looking so handsome."

Duncan saw the mischievous light in her eye. "All right, Weasel, I will." He gave her an impulsive hug, remembering suddenly the springtime party in this house over two years back.

No, it would not all be magic for Sally, or for Raymond either. They too would suffer from the snubs, and worse. He kissed her quickly,

217

stood and started down the stairs. Growing up in all this, could she ever go back to her grandmother's teepee or even the Great Hall at Ile-à-la-Crosse?

The music and voices and the gaiety and laughter. MacGillivray père snatching glasses from a passing tray. The kings and princes of the fur trade, their wives and daughters, the dowagers and damsels, the society of all Montreal. Ah. There was Marianne looking up at her tall blond officer, her hand resting on his and. . .here was Gilles.

"Duncan, my old friend!" He came bounding up the stairs, gripping his hand, pumping it hard. "It's good to see you, Duncan. Come along. I'm late. Follow me."

He led the way to his room with quick strides. "We'll talk while I change. Come on, sit down. Have some wine. There's a decanter over there. And pour me some, will you? The sherry. . ." He tugged at his stock and his shirt buttons. "You've a lot to tell me, eh?" He rummaged in his chest of drawers, pulling out clean linen, tossing it on the bed. "I know, you've made a thousand pounds in furs and you've come to Montreal to spend it." He laughed in that quick bursting way he had. To Gilles the world was his and life was a gift to be enjoyed.

"No, Gilles. The opposite, in fact. But never mind. You look as though the world is treating you well."

Gilles was tall and lean. His mobile face and

intense dark eyes had even more of his father about them. The old vitality was there, and the sense of fun and adventure that had got them into so many scrapes.

"Oh, yes," Gilles said, "I've been doing fine. I want to get up to le pays d'en haut, though. Montreal's all very well, but. . . Here, help me with this stock, will you. . .finger on the knot. Yes, I should spend two or three winters, really get to know the trade. Like you, you rascal."

Gilles' clothes were expensive, even the every-day suit he had stripped off and left in a heap. He pulled a pair of gleaming black shoes from his armoire. "That great whale, Wee Willie Mac-Gillivray, was all over me downstairs. You'd think he was Peter Pond and Alec Mackenzie and David Thompson rolled into one. He's not going back, of course. Crowing because he'll get into the Beaver Club before me."

"I'm sure he learned a thing or two and he's peeled off some blubber. He couldn't help it, being with Fergus Macdonald," Duncan said.

"Yes. I hear that old rogue came down with the MacGillivray brigade for his furlough and he's looking for a bride. Look out, ladies! Look out, Montreal! Anyway, Duncan, we should go in business together, you know."

He looked up from tying his shoelace. "Remember how we used to talk about the day we'd take over when the old men retired? Your father's retiring, I hear. He'll pass his share to you?"

"I don't know about that," Duncan said carefully. "I'd be a partner with you in anything, Gilles, but I. . .may not go back."

"May not go back?" Gilles stopped, his hairbrush poised, looking at his friend in the mirror. "But we always talked about it. When we were this high. Remember? Cameron and Letellier all over. And you were going to marry Marianne, and I was going to marry some beautiful Indian princess." He laughed. "Maybe that's not such a bad idea. Know any beautiful Indian princesses?"

"There are things you probably haven't heard, Gilles." Duncan's voice was serious, and Gilles turned to face him.

"I've heard more than you think. That affair at Ile-à-la-Crosse, you mean?"

"And other things. But it all started with that."

"Look. You never have to apologize or explain to a friend. But the story I hear is that Duncan Cameron got distracted by a girl who'd been set up as a decoy, there was shooting and an engagé got killed. Then Angus Cameron rapped your knuckles by sending you off to Lac la Ronge. He burned down the Hudson's Bay fort. Another victory for the North West Company. Finis. Right?"

"It was far more than a knuckle-rapping, Gilles." Duncan shook his head, lips tight. "But that's something like it."

"Imagine, a rascal like you being taken in by a girl!" Gilles grinned, trying to ease the tension. "Was she worth it, eh?"

"Stop it, Gilles! Stop it!" Duncan could feel

the muscle working in his jaw. "The whole world's heard something about this. Everyone puts his own picture on it. The canoemen up there call me a traitor who threw away a good man's life. As far as most people are concerned, I'm a damned fool taken in by some girl. My own father says I betrayed my trust. So that makes me no longer a gentleman — if I ever damned well was one. They won't renew my trading licence, so I'm on my own."

He paused, breathing hard, looking straight into Gilles' eyes. His voice dropped as his anger grew. "And the partners, of course, say what they always say. About half-breeds. I know. . .I know what they say when they don't think I can hear. Can't really count on 'em, can you? Not the same as us, are they? Mongrels, really. Like the dogs who saved my life, Gilles. Not pure-bred Scots and French and English and spaniels and race horses and. . ."

"Duncan, now *you* stop!"

"Face it, Gilles, would a half-breed be good enough for Marianne?"

"Why don't you ask her yourself, goddamn it?" Gilles bit off the words and the two of them stood glaring, toe to toe.

The fire popped. The sound of music intruded from below. Gilles finally grated, "Look, my friend, you're in no mood to play Beau Brummel down there with all that lot. Marianne's flirting with her hoity-toity English officer. The other girls are a lot of puddings. Why don't we leave them to Wee Willie? Let's you and me go down to Gabriel's and some of those other old places."

He picked up his cloak and put his hand on Duncan's shoulder. "We'll slip down the back stairs and pick up a calêche. If it's the only way to get that chip off your shoulder and that scowl off your rotten brown face, we'll drink 'em off. What d'you say to that? Eh, half-breed?"

"Thanks, Gilles." Duncan looked at his friend. "I needed that. And if I get drunk enough, I might tell you about the girl. You know, the only men who have never judged me on all this are my grandfather and you."

"We have a lot in common. You know something I found out not so long ago? My father's grandmother was a Cree."

19
Chez le Boeuf

Gabriel's was jam-packed. Everyone tonight was celebrating the arrival of the fall brigades. The upper crust were at soirées like the Letelliers'. Family folk had parties in their homes. The bachelor clerks and the apprentices were howling around the better taverns of the town. Canoemen caroused in their own favourite haunts.

Gabriel's was among the more respectable. It was shaking, nonetheless, with shouts and ribald song. Young men jammed into every corner. A lively lot of pretty barmaids worked their way through the crowd with trays. Word was that they were all members of la famille Gabriel, and anyone who treated them in an unseemly way would be banned forever by M'sieu. To be banned from Gabriel's was the junior clerk's equivalent of being suspended from the Beaver Club.

"There's Logan," Gilles bellowed above the noise. "And Douglas and that rogue. . ."

"Emery?"

"That's his name. Let's join them."

Emery looked up. His pocked face was flushed as usual and his knobby nose glowed. "Gad! If it ain't young Duncan Cameron — and Gilles Letellier. Come sit down. You know Baldwin and all?"

Emery had spent eight years failing his apprenticeship. Then he'd run through a decent inheritance from his fur-trader father. He had a good measure of cunning, conviviality to spare, and a complete absence of scruples.

Tonight he was well into his role as chief buffoon, entertaining all concerned with the latest shady story, starting off a song, drinking everything that came in reach and paying for none.

He nudged Duncan. "What's this I hear, young fella? Been cut off by your father. Little trouble with a lady, was it?"

"Something like that." You couldn't take offence at the man somehow.

"Never mind. If you're pitched out o' the family firm, old Emery could bring a bit o' business your way. We could incorporate. Half-breeds & Co. You know — 'We do the dirty work, you keep your hands clean.' How would that suit? Us bits o' brown should stick together, Cameron. The big trouble real gentlemen have is integrity, honour, that sort of thing. Gets in the way. But not us, eh?" He winked, jerked out a beery laugh and waved an arm. "Here, have a drink. Chantal. . .hey, Chantal!"

He tipped his hat forward and began to lead 'Alouette.' He was halfway through the tenth chorus when Chantal came back with the drinks. As expected, Duncan paid.

More stories, more gossip, more drink. Duncan swirled the dregs in his glass. If he came back to this, maybe he'd be just another Emery.

A fellow with a fine baritone was singing from a table top. He finished to applause, then struck up again.

"Ah, si mon moine voulait danser. . ."

The crowd roared back the response.

"Un capuchon je lui donnerais. . ."

The song leaped along to the rhythm of the child and the spinning top — the reluctant dancing monk. Imaginary paddles were wielded, the choruses rang out and echoed back. It was the rhythm of the paddles now, and it was the voice of Ti'moine Tremblay, and the ceiling was the early-morning sky.

> *"Danse mon moine, danse!*
> *Tu n'entend pas la danse. . ."*

Ti'moine Tremblay — the finest songster maybe in the whole northwest. Ti'moine singing down that last long stretch to Ile-à-la-Crosse, singing and plying his paddle. Racing to be home first. Home to dance with his family. Home. And that was the last time he ever did it in his life. . . .

Suddenly the room was insufferably hot. Duncan dropped his glass on the table and pushed his way through the roistering crowd to the door.

"Duncan. There you are, you rascal!" Gilles burst out of Gabriel's behind a couple of others who tottered off singing.

"Just came out for some air, Gilles, and a change of scene." Duncan was leaning against the wall.

"All right, mon ami. Whatever you say. Wherever you say. Where'll we go? Rascoe's? It's very modern."

"Let's try le Boeuf's." Duncan stepped off along the pavement.

"Oho! After the girls, is Duncan." Gilles caught up. "Whatever you say, Casanova. There are better places, but it's your night." He flung his arm over Duncan's shoulder and they headed down Saint-Gabriel towards the port.

Girls. If that was what Gilles thought, all right. Chez le Boeuf was where every voyageur alive went to drink in Montreal. It was the place where they would catch up with each other, where company agents would find them, get them drunk and sign them on. It was the place where they could spend the better part of a year's wages on liquor and ladies and dice before staggering off with a thick head to swagger about their home parish for the off-season.

Ti'moine Tremblay had had a brother. He'd referred to him with some contempt as a maudit mangeur de lard who would give no help to their poor old parents. If Duncan could find him, though, he might find the parents. It had come home to him back there at Gabriel's that they, at least, deserved a visit from the one who had seen their staunch son die. Chez le Boeuf was the place for gossip. He might even find the brother there.

And Chez le Boeuf was roaring. You could hear it as you turned into rue Saint-Paul. The doors and windows were open, which mercifully let in some fresh air, but even at that the smoke, the stench and the din under the low-beamed ceiling were overpowering. Bright feathers in coloured hats. Brown faces, flashing teeth, raised tankards, singing. Potboys dodging through the tables. Girls dancing between them — and on them. Here and there an unconscious form curled up beneath.

Duncan shouted, "Let's have a word with le Boeuf."

The proprietor must have had another name, but no one knew it. He was a great ox of a man, looming over the bar counter at the back. He towered over most of his customers, which was useful when it came time to keep some kind of order. At his size, he could never have been hired as a voyageur, so he'd probably not been west of Lachine. In spite of that, he knew who and where everybody in the fur trade might be at any time.

"M'sieu Letellier, bon soir... Oho, M'sieu Cameron, heh? A long time."

"Oui, le Boeuf. Two years... More," Duncan said.

"And plenty happens up there in le pays d'en

haut, eh, m'sieu?" He laughed and his chins and belly shook and his shrewd eyes disappeared into the folds of his face. "What will you drink tonight, messieurs?"

"Lots, le Boeuf. Lots." Gilles laughed. "Your best Jamaica for us both."

Duncan said, "Do you know a Tremblay? Un mangeur de lard, I think."

"Tremblay? There are hundreds. I've seen Felix and Ferdinand and Louis and. . ."

"This one has a brother — un homme du nord — called Theophile — Ti'moine."

"Oho, that Ti'moine who is dead, eh?" A sideways look. "The brother is Armand then, from Saint-Sulpice. You are looking for him?" His little eyes took on a vaguely clouded look.

"I am, le Boeuf. I owe the family something. I'd be much obliged." Duncan found half a Spanish dollar in his pocket and slid it onto the counter. It disappeared in a ham-like hand.

"Pas problème, m'sieu. . ."

A song led by a merry-sounding fiddle ended. A roar of applause, the fiddler plinked his strings and launched another tune. A couple of hearties shoved back a table and began a step dance. Someone rattled a pair of spoons. Another joined in. The rest began to whoop, beating time with their tankards on the table tops. More stood and moved in to watch.

Duncan climbed on his chair to see over the tops of their heads and clapped to the rhythm. The little fiddler backed towards him to make

228

more room for the dancers. The spoons clattered crazily. The fiddle bow worked faster, faster, faster. The clapping increased. Shouts urged the dancers on. The fiddler worked the pitch up — and the pace — higher, higher, higher. A final whoop from the dancers. It was over.

The crowd yelled for more but the dancers tottered to their seats, reached out for drink. The fiddler flourished his bow, took off his flop-brimmed hat to collect his tips.

Duncan jumped down from his chair and gulped his rum. "He deserves something."

"He does." Gilles laughed and produced a coin. "Here, add this to yours."

Duncan elbowed through the crush. "Hey. Violoniste! Well played, fiddler. Here." He reached over the table with his coins.

The hat swung towards the sound of his voice. The shabby little man stepped closer. Wispy hair, a blind man's darkened glasses, smiling face. He turned it up to Duncan's and. . .he froze. For just one instant.

"M'sieu." A hoarse whisper. "Merci, m'sieu." He turned away.

Suddenly the smoky lamps were a glowing fire. The sounds of the crowd were rushing water and wind in the pines. The table between them was the bottom of an overturned canoe. There was a musket pointing at him. And the face. . .

"Coco Pinet!"

Duncan leaped. He sprawled half across the table. Tankards clattered. Someone shouted. He clawed for the little man and missed. The face. Smoked glasses or no.

"Pinet!"

He lunged again. The table tipped. Duncan tumbled to the floor. A welter of mugs and ale and rum and clattering chairs. Table legs, feet. Cheers, shouts, curses.

He scrambled up. A hand clamped his arm. "Hey, m'sieu, quoi. . .?" He knocked the man aside. Pinet. Where was he? He whirled. Faces all around. Angry. Shouting. Laughing. Drunk.

They ringed him in. He took one look and charged. Head down, he burst straight through, tripped, half fell. He saw a small figure, scuttling off. Past the tables, near the bar.

A fiercely grinning face in front. He hammered it aside. Someone grabbed him from behind. Down he went again.

"Let go, blast you!" He flailed behind.

"Attention!" A roar from overhead. There was Gilles, plucking the man from his back, and he was free.

"Come on!" Duncan yelled. He charged for the bar. He jumped a table, hurdled a froth of petticoats, knocked a potboy flying.

Le Boeuf's huge bulk was disappearing through the swinging doors. Duncan slammed after him. It was the kitchen — cluttered, smoky. Screams from serving girls. Clatter of pots and pans. A mighty roar from the giant le Boeuf, standing at the outside door.

Duncan dodged a girl who dropped her trayful, then he ran square into the chopping block.

A great meat cleaver was stuck in it. He grasped its handle, tugged it out.

Then he charged past le Boeuf, half slipped on the garbage-strewn cobbles. A cat screeched and ran.

"That way. . ." Le Boeuf was pointing.

Duncan saw a figure at the end of the alley turning into the street. He was after him. Under a lamp Pinet dodged through a gaggle of tipsy sailors. They saw Duncan's cleaver, scattered and cheered him as he pounded by.

Shuttered windows. Dark. He turned the next corner. The street narrowed down and jigged. Dark doorways either side, a slit of starlit sky above. Ahead, the wall went right across. The cul-de-sac behind rue Saint-Joseph. He had him now. He had him trapped.

He must be in the dark somewhere. He'd see him if he tried to climb the wall. If he were in one of those doorways. . . These damned shoes made so much noise. Moccasins were. . .

A whispered sound. A rush. A glint of steel. Someone came at him like a demon. He slipped to one knee, turned. The man flipped across his back, hit the cobbles with a gasp. Duncan saw him rise and crouch, glimpsed the knife, heard his indrawn breath.

Then he bounded forward, lashed out with his foot, caught him on the kneecap. The man went down.

Duncan raised the cleaver. "I'll cut you in half, you. . ."

"Non, m'sieu. Non." A clatter and the knife

231

fell. The man sagged forward. "For Jesus' sake, m'sieu." He crossed himself, then his arms covered his head.

"Where is he? Tell me. Tell me or I'll do it. Where's Whistler? Where's the Wolverine? Where is he, I say?"

Footsteps hammered on the paving. A single shout. "Duncan!"

"Here, Gilles. Over here. I've got him." He didn't take his eyes from Pinet for a second.

"What the devil's going on, Duncan? Have you gone crazy?" Gilles' footsteps slowed. He was blowing hard. "And who the hell's that?"

"An old friend of mine. Coco Pinet. He's a murderer. Remember it, Coco?" He reached down, grabbed the front of Coco's shirt, jerked him up and slammed him back against the wall. He held the cleaver right in front of the man's face.

"Remember, Coco? Will you remember when you die? Will you remember it in hell? The devil will remember."

"I didn't. I swear to the Holy Virgin. M'sieu Cameron — I never killed. Believe me. . ." He crossed himself again.

"You were with Whistler, weren't you? At Lac la Ronge."

"I stayed with the canoe. It was Whistler killed the man. And burned the place."

"So you were there. You're guilty too."

"It was only him, those others. Not me. Ask him, m'sieu. Ask him yourself."

"Where is he then?" He raised the cleaver.

"Here, m'sieu. Right here in Montreal."

"Here?. . ." Duncan's racing mind jolted. The rage moved back. Instead, he turned ice-cold.

"I don't believe you, Coco. You're a liar, as you always were. You die right now."

"I swear. I swear it on the cross."

"Then why did he come to Montreal? Why?" Hudson's Bay men didn't come to Montreal, except their agents, some deserters, men in trouble.

"He killed a man. Isbister. He was drunk and he killed him. So he went to St. Paul in the States. He paid me just to paddle."

"Go on."

"Then he needed money. He came here to see the agent."

"Coco Pinet." Duncan's voice was measured, deadly. "You are taking us to Harry Whistler now. Right now. One wrong step, one whisper of warning, and I'll split your head like a turnip." He paused for it to sink in. "And your black soul, Coco, will fry in hell forever."

Without moving his eyes, he said coldly, "His knife's on the ground, Gilles. If he tries anything at all," he lowered the cleaver, took a half pace back, "kill him."

20
Rue Saint-Louis

They walked westward along rue Saint-Paul with Pinet sandwiched between them. Each held a knife point hard against his ribs.

"Why do you travel with him?" Duncan snapped.

"If I don't, he'll kill me," Pinet whined. "Only because he needs me, I stay alive. He's a mad dog. He drinks and drinks. His money is nearly gone."

"Is he going to stay here? In Montreal?"

"When he gets more money he says Albany, New York, somewhere. . . ."

Darkened warehouses glowered at them from the dockside. Through the shadowed slits between them they could see the masts and spars of ships etched against the stars. If Whistler got past Montreal, he might comb the world for him forever.

Gilles shot, "Why did he let you out tonight, crapaud?"

"He's drunk, m'sieu. Dead drunk. Me, I have

no money. I go out to make some with my violin. If I can make enough. . ."

"You'll dump him, eh?" Gilles growled. "Why not just rob him when he's drunk? It's likely more your style."

"M'sieu?. . ."

"All's well." The measured cry came from the other side of Place d'Armes. Pinet jumped at the shout. It was the watch.

Duncan jabbed him hard. "You'll get no help from them," he hissed.

"Two o'clock. All's well." The echoing voice receded.

They slipped through the square by the French Church. There was not a soul about. Pinet pointed to a narrow street ahead.

"Rue Saint-Louis?" Gilles gave his arm a twist. Pinet sucked his breath and nodded.

"Number? What number?"

He shook his head. He must know. Was he trying some trick? More likely he was terrified he'd lose his wretched life as soon as they found their major prey.

Narrow street, darkened doorways, shuttered windows, littered cobbles. A solitary lamp cast a weak circle of light at the first corner. Run-down, narrow houses with alleys in between. Steep-pitched roofs above, blank-eyed dormers. . . .

Pinet stopped, pointed to a dingy door.

"Number seventeen?" Duncan whispered. "Which room?"

Pinet motioned towards the slit of an alley at

the side. Duncan raised the cleaver. "You go first. I'm right behind with this."

For the first few yards they had to turn sideways to get through. Then it opened out a little. Duncan stepped carefully over rubbish, keeping the back of a hand on either wall. Rats squeaked and scuttled. Ahead a cat yowled briefly.

The houses here were narrow but this one ran back over fifty feet. It ended abruptly and the night with its starlit sky seemed almost bright. An eight-foot wall continued beyond the house and disappeared into some sort of lane behind. Rotting garbage stank.

A low gate in the wall loomed dark. Pinet motioned, put his finger to his lips. He pulled the latch firmly towards him first, then lifted hard to take the weight off squeaky hinges before he pushed it in.

They were in a tiny yard, three walls. On the other side, the house — with one dark doorway, shuttered windows.

Duncan hissed in Pinet's ear. "Which room, and how do I get there? If you lie to me or make a noise, it will be your last."

Pinet pointed upwards to the second floor. The end window on the right showed a tiny slit of light. Then he pointed to the door. "Kitchen," he whispered. "Go right, upstairs, then right again."

Duncan felt Gilles' hand on his arm. He spoke very quietly. "Duncan, what are you going to do?"

"Kill Whistler." His own voice sounded like a thunderclap. There was no question in his mind.

"But you can't. That's for the hangman. We know where Whistler is. I'll fetch the watch. They'll arrest him. He'll hang."

Back in the reaches of Duncan's mind he heard a voice again, a strong old voice: The Wolverine will die for his crimes, and you will see that it is so. . . . Once, he had allowed himself to be turned aside. But not again. He shook his head.

Gilles pressed. "This is Canada, Duncan, not the northwest. Mad as it is, if you kill him like that, they could hang *you*."

"I know." He pulled Gilles out of Pinet's earshot. "I know, Gilles. Look, you take this maggot somewhere so far away I'll never find him again. If I do, I'll kill him too. I'll go away — somewhere in the States. I'll write to you. Please try to get the word to Cut Hand and my mother. Tell them I'll go back home someday. Good-bye, my friend. Go now. Good-bye."

Pinet held out a heavy latch key and motioned to the door.

The sound of Medicine Rapid was in Duncan's ears. "One last thing, Pinet," he said. "Is he alone?"

"Oui, m'sieu. He is alone."

The key turned in the lock with a rusty crunch. Duncan pushed the door in slightly, felt warm air on his cheek. Smell of stale boiled cabbage, smoke, rancid fat. He listened. Nothing. He held his breath. He opened the door wide to let in all the light he could.

Across the room a tiny ruby glow. Kitchen stove, the fire near dead. Flagged floor underfoot. He stooped and untied his shoes, carefully took them off, knotted the laces, slung them around his neck.

He crept along the wall. The cleaver hung heavy in his hand. It was as good a weapon as any. Dead was dead. It didn't matter how. But his stomach turned.

The stairs. His stockinged toe came up against the bottom riser. The wall was on the right, no banister on the open side. The stairway rose, turned left.

Feet felt out each tread. Above him it was darker. The stairway turned again, rose through blackness to the floor above. A banister rail around the stairwell. A hall. Turn right now, to the end. And that door there — that door is Whistler's.

A slit of light beneath the door. His left hand on the knob, the weapon in his right. Now. Move in, kill, get out. All with silent speed.

He turned the knob. It made no sound. He pushed the door inwards very softly. One lamp on a bureau casting shadows. Not much light. Enough, though. Just enough. He glided in. His stockinged feet felt bare, uneven planks. The room was stuffy, close. It reeked of liquor. He heard breathing — harsh, uneven, deep. A bed against the other wall.

In the corner. . .half covered, face down-wards, one shirt-sleeved arm lolling, fingers nearly to the floor. Whistler. Sodden. The arrogant Harry Whistler, a helpless drunk.

A chair was lying on its side, clothes strewn about. He only had to see the face close up. To be quite sure. No mistake. He must make no mistake. He slid one foot ahead, then the next, testing every step. A pool of darkness by the bed. The breathing rasped on. He was very near.

His toe hit something hard. It moved, rolled. An earthquake rumbling right across the floor. It was a bottle, rolling, rolling. . . .

Clink! It stopped.

"Arrrrh!" The figure stirred. An arm came up. He flopped over on his back. Whistler. Not the slightest doubt. The straight nose, high forehead, contemptuous twist to the lips — even now.

Duncan's arm rose. Up, up it came, the cleaver heavy in his hand. Heavy as an executioner's axe. The face on the bed turned upwards now. Duncan felt a growl rising in his throat.

"Wolverine!" his voice rasped out. The wretch must see him as he died.

Whistler's face now caught the light. His eyes blinked open, besotted, dazed. He tried to sit, tugging something from the blanket. Duncan saw him yank the pistol free, swing it up towards him. He saw the face contort. The other hand came up to help. He heard a gasp, saw the mouth drop open, saw the terror in his eyes.

239

His own arm was moving now. The grisly weapon swung downwards in a monstrous arc, right for Whistler's head.

And. . .he turned his hand. The cleaver struck — blade flat. He felt the jar right up his arm. He saw Whistler's eyes glaze, his jaw sag. He saw him slump sideways, slide halfway to the floor, roll over on his back. The pistol lay beside his hand.

Duncan looked at the cleaver. The blood was the dried remnant left there by the butcher at le Boeuf's. He stooped, put a hand on Whistler's chest. The man was breathing.

He was too weary then to even hold the cleaver. He let it fall. He wanted no more of this. No more of killing. No more blood. Slowly he went to the window. He unlatched the shutters, threw them wide. Air rushed in, clean and cold. He sucked his lungs full, closed his eyes for a long moment. His chin dropped on his chest. His stomach gave a silent heave. Bile rose halfway up his throat. He retched, clamped his teeth and swallowed hard, breathed more cold air.

He looked out the window at the star-filled sky, the line of roofs, the pool of black below. What had he done? What had he left undone? How far away was Gilles?

"Gilles!" he tried to shout. The name would scarcely come. "Gilles!"

"Duncan! Yes!" The voice was right below

240

the window. He had not left. He had not moved. His friend had stayed to help.

"Come up, Gilles. Come on up, mon ami. And bring Pinet. We have more vermin up here for the garbage heap."

He leaned back against the wall, sweat running on his face and neck. He could feel it trickling down his chest. He shivered with the cold. Outside, the cat screeched. There were distant sounds inside the house.

Feet pounded on the stairs and up above. Voices sounded in the passage, getting louder. More light reached the doorway. The twisted figure on the floor stirred. The head half lifted and with a moan dropped back.

Duncan's eyes never left that semi-conscious form. He heard his own voice say, "Forgive me, Grandfather. I did not kill him. Forgive me. I'm not a man like you."

21
On Trial

"How do you plead?"

The clerk peered over his glasses at Whistler standing in the dock. Not a sound came from the crowded courtroom. The judge balanced his chin on the tips of his fingers and pursed his narrow lips.

Whistler looked squarely up at him. "Not guilty, my lord, on any of the charges." He was pale but he stood erect and seemingly relaxed. His lips curled slightly. His voice was firm, his clothes impeccable.

Whispers whisked about the room like dry leaves. He was a good-looking man, Whistler, well-groomed, well-spoken. He had a cultivated accent. A gentleman, certainly. A murderer too? The twelve jurymen shifted in their seats. Clerks scribbled, wigged counsel shuffled papers, muttered. Duncan's mouth went dry.

The seats behind him were filled. Fergus Macdonald was there. So were the Letelliers — except for Marianne.

"Maître Gelinas?" The judge's eyes were all that moved. They swung to the crown prosecutor.

"Indeed, my lord." Gelinas was a dapper, precise little man with knowing eyes. "The crown, my lord, will show. . ."

The trial began. Witnesses were called. Fergus Macdonald gave a graphic account of hostilities in the northwest. The Hudson's Bay Company had been losing ground for years. Now they were trying to bully their way back into the trade by sending in young firebrands like Whistler. He read Angus Cameron's letter telling of the courier Quick Feet's murder and the warrant for Whistler's arrest. Another letter told of Whistler's disappearance from Ile-à-la-Crosse.

Then Duncan told what had happened out on the ice that January day.

"The man's face had been totally shot away at close range," he said. Every grisly detail was etched in his mind. "Whistler claimed the man was dead when he arrived but he called him a northern Indian. . . ."

"And could you tell the court the significance of that?"

"Yes, sir. The northern Indians — Chipewyans and Slavey and others — they have distinctly different features from the Cree. But there was nothing left of the man's face. . . ."

Then there were the toboggan tracks. His own, coming up the lake. The express toboggan's coming down. Whistler's from Kazan Lake, then up the trail. No others.

"Whistler's men beat me unconscious. When I came around, I followed their trail up beside the creek. They had gone half a mile and camped where they could watch the lake. No one else could have killed that man. Unless he flew."

Then he told the story of Hunter Bay. All seemed well until he faced Whistler's counsel, a deceptively ponderous man with a double chin and heavy-lidded eyes.

"Mr. Cameron, on this particular winter Sunday you were, I understand. . .ah, joy-riding with Miss Nancy Spence in a dog sled. Would you tell the court what relationship you had with Miss Spence."

Question after clever question. With every answer, a picture grew. Duncan saw it being painted, stroke by stroke. He sensed the doubt growing in the jury's minds.

"And when you first met Mr. Whistler, you were over visiting Miss Spence?"

"I had been to see her father. She was showing me to the counting house."

"Mr. Whistler had you ejected from the fort. Did you resent that?"

"Naturally, sir. It was not called for."

"You and Mr. Whistler argued over dancing with Miss Spence?"

"Yes, but. . ."

"You took her out in the toboggan even though her father had forbidden it?"

"She had been told not to see me — yes."

The lawyer paused. "Now, Mr. Cameron, when

did you find out that Miss Spence and Whistler were living as man and wife?"

Man and wife. Duncan's throat closed so that he could barely speak. The night scene flooded his mind once more. He heard the sound of water. He managed, "When I caught up with him at Medicine Rapid."

"A young Indian had told you someone of Whistler's description had killed his parents. Tell me, how old was the boy?"

"Six years old."

"Six years old! And on the word of a six-year-old you paddled a hundred miles and risked your own life to try to avenge some Indians' deaths?" The lawyer's face and voice spoke contemptuous disbelief. "No, sir. Harry Whistler happened to have taken the girl you wanted for yourself. That, sir, is why you sought revenge."

Duncan didn't answer. He could not undo the damage. He walked stiffly to his chair, feeling mistrust in every eye.

"Jacques Pinet!"

Coco, brought in by prison guards, was his old neat self. Cartwright, the long-faced assistant crown attorney, had seen to it that he had respectable clothes. He kept rotating his cap in his hands and gave an ingratiating smile each time he answered Gelinas' questions.

"Oui, m'sieu. That M'sieu Whistler, he was our bourgeois. We paddled all the way from Green Lake to Hunter Bay to fix this Duncan Cameron. I saw Whistler with my own eyes shoot the Indian dead. With a pistol. Right there by the shore. The woman locked herself in the house, firing muskets, so Whistler gives the orders and the place begins to burn. . . ."

Coco seemed almost to enjoy telling it. His story was sickeningly clear. The interpreter gave an English version for the learned judge and others who required it.

"Me, I stay in the canoe, as I am told. For a long time it burns. I hear her screams." He paused. "Then M'sieu Whistler comes down and says, 'That does for Cameron's brown bitch, and his mongrel pup.' "

An indrawn gasp came from somewhere in the crowd. Whistler's brief gesture to his counsel dismissed it as a pack of lies.

"Whistler believed then that the woman had been Duncan Cameron's wife?"

"No, m'sieu. He thought it was his mother. Angus Cameron's wife. We all thought that was so. But no one saw the woman. She was inside the cabin."

Whistler's counsel barely cross-examined Pinet. Instead, he called a leathery-faced staunch old guide who spoke with personal knowledge on Coco Pinet's reliability — or lack of it. "A fine fiddler, m'sieu. The very best there is. But. . ."

Brisk answers to a few well-phrased questions, and Pinet stood branded as a shirker, a liar and a thief.

Cartwright whispered to Duncan, "The jury

246

won't believe him now. Unless someone speaks in his favour."

"Who would?" Duncan shook his head. "That old fellow's dead right."

Court was adjourned for the day. Duncan ate a cold supper in Cartwright's chambers and they thrashed gloomily through the case for the hundredth time. Then he walked some distance through the silent streets in the sharp night air to clear his head. It was very late when he got back to Maison Letellier.

"Have some coffee, Duncan — or some brandy. You look worn out." Gilles met him at the door and led him to the library. There was a fire burning and a tray in front of it.

"My parents are in bed," said Gilles. "They send their best wishes. They're on your side, Duncan. Whatever."

"And Marianne?"

"Oh," Gilles tried to be offhand. "Some officers' picnic tomorrow. Her dressmaker. . . But how's it going, d'you think?"

"The lawyers are worried. With Pinet pretty well discredited, it's my word against Whistler's. There are just no other witnesses."

"Well then, it's a Nor'wester versus the Bay." Gilles shrugged. "That makes it easy. The jurymen are all Montrealers. Company men or not, they know who butters their bread."

"And it's half-breed against white too. That works the other way."

"Duncan, forget that, damn it," Gilles growled. "If it's more witnesses we need, what about the other voyageurs?"

"They'd all hang with Whistler if they showed up." Duncan shook his head. "And the northwest is a big place to hide."

"What about Nancy Spence then?"

"What about her?" Duncan bit off the words.

"Well, she was with you right after Quick Feet was killed. She heard what Whistler said. She must have seen what happened at Hunter Bay too."

Duncan's jaw tightened. "God, yes, she must have." And still she'd gone on with him. He could feel the cheek muscles working. He said harshly, "She's his wife. Doesn't that mean she can't give evidence. . .even if we could find her?"

A long silence. Finally Duncan jerked out a dry laugh. "So much for Nancy Spence. And so much for the law. Gilles, the way it looks right now, Whistler could get off. I should have killed him. Twice I should have killed him. Cut Hand sees it right, you know. It's our business. Our family's affair. It's got nothing to do with white men or the law or this ridiculous trial. This. . ."

He looked into the fire. "Two chances. I had two chances at Whistler. When it came right down to it, Gilles, I was just too damned chicken-hearted. Now if he gets off, all I can do is wait for him on the courthouse steps with a pistol."

"Don't be a fool. You'll be hanged instead of him."

"How else will my grandfather ever rest easy? Or the others in my family? Or me?...How else?"

Whistler's counsel summed up his defence. It was formidable. "How many renegade Indians could have had an opportunity to murder the courier Quick Feet? How much reliance can be placed in sled tracks on the snow? Is a fire at a trading post such an unusual event? What iota of proof is there that the unfortunate woman and her child did not die by accident? Could any of Mr. Cameron's statements be corroborated?"

Each question was a hammer blow. Here was an erratic young half-breed who'd been turfed out by his own father for dereliction of duty. Here was the hot-blooded youth, chasing a native lass and losing her to a mature, responsible, well-placed gentleman. Here was the jealous young failure who tried to kill his rival — at Medicine Rapid, and then again in Montreal. Having failed twice, he built a web of lies in cahoots with the shiftless Pinet...

"Certainly there was bad blood between the accused and young Mr. Cameron. They were rivals for the same girl. And Harry Whistler won." The counsel turned his sleepy gaze towards the jury box. "But the gentlemen of the jury know full well, my lord, that the accused is not on trial for the seduction of a half-breed girl — a not-altogether-unusual occurrence. He's on trial for murder. They will find the case against Mr.

Whistler to be a total fabrication. . . ."

Duncan saw the expressions of the jury, triumph and contempt on Whistler's face. He heard the hum of talk. He heard his name being whispered. He felt the lashing of a hundred tongues. He forced himself to turn around and caught the eyes of Gilles, Raymond Letellier and his wife. Alone they said, We are with you. We are with you. . . .

There was one other. Fergus Macdonald. He looked straight at Duncan with his eagle's eyes narrowed and he nodded, firmly, twice. Then he clenched his fist at Whistler. Marianne Letellier? She must be at her picnic.

What more was to be done? The judge would sum up. Then the jury would go out. There seemed to be some stirring at the crown attorney's table, some moving to and fro. But for all that counted, it was over. Whistler would get off.

What sense did all this make? Here they were, these learned folk with all their stately, ordered ritual, deciding what had happened some other time, some other place, three thousand miles away. They sat here in this stone courthouse in their English wigs and gowns, in their London-fashion clothes, pretending that they understood — that it was their God-given right to judge — that they *knew*.

Maître Gelinas was hunched before the judge with some papers in his hand. More posturing. More lawyer's talk.

Brilliant men, no doubt. But how many of

them had even laid eyes on that land, let alone come to understand it? How many of them had ever followed a winter trail with dogs, or slept in a smoky teepee, or hunted for their food, or understood what happened between people and the land, people and each other? With all the logic of their own law, had they even talked to one who really knew?

He felt a hand on his shoulder. Gilles? He shook his head. He didn't really want to talk. The hand persisted. He looked up. Not Gilles. No. It was his father. It was Angus Cameron. He had come back to Montreal.

Duncan felt completely empty. He had no wish to see his father. He would speak to him with Sally and Raymond, as he had planned. That was all. He made himself look up again. His father's face was drawn and lined. His eyes were keen clear blue, though, under the heavy brows, and his jaw was firm, as always. The hand stayed on his shoulder as he rose. What now? What was he to say? The lady. The Edinburgh lady. Was she here?

He looked towards the public seats. The Letelliers. She would be with them. But there was no stranger. Only Fergus Macdonald, Sally and Raymond.

"Duncan, my son, we have a good deal to say to one another." Crooked Nose turned towards him. "Let us sit down together." Those first words that he spoke were Cree.

Slowly Duncan sat. His father took the chair

beside him. Low-voiced he said, "Magnus Spence brought me the news. You'll hear. . ."

"May it please the court. . ." The crown attorney's voice struggled above the talk.

"Order." The judge rapped his gavel. "Order." In his acid tones he said, "Maître Gelinas, you have evidence you wish to introduce. Pray, make it brief."

"You have before you, my lord, letters that have just come into my possession." Gelinas referred to his notes. "One is dated 17th October last year near Frog Portage in the Indian country. It is franked at Fort Churchill and was carried in the autumn vessel out of Hudson Bay to a Mr. Magnus Spence at Stromness — that is in the Orkney Islands, I believe."

"Letters!" Duncan whispered to his father. "Did you bring them here?"

Cameron nodded. "Old Magnus came to me in Edinburgh in December."

Gelinas went on. "There is also a sworn statement from Mr. Spence and a bundle of letters signed by Mr. Fergus Macdonald from Fort Chipewyan. Mr. Spence testifies that he found these letters in Mr. Whistler's possession at Ile-à-la-Crosse after the robbing of the express."

A flurry of whispers. The clerk collected the letters from the judge and moved over to Whistler in the dock.

Gelinas spoke quietly. "I would like you to look carefully at that letter, Mr. Whistler — the one written from Frog Portage last October. Tell us if it was written by you."

Whistler put out his hand, then pulled it back. His face was the colour of ash. He said not a word.

"To refresh Mr. Whistler's mind, my lord, I will read a short portion of that letter, addressed to Mr. Spence." Gelinas held his hand out and the clerk brought it over. He read:

> . . . .You will be pleased to hear that the burning of Ile-à-la-Crosse is avenged. Just two days ago I saw the North West post at Hunter Bay burn to the ground with all its contents. It was run by that mischief-making half-breed cur, Duncan Cameron, and the contents included Angus Cameron's squaw called Rose Flower and her latest small brown bastard.

A sigh blew through the courtroom like a hot wind before a storm.

> . . . .I am sure, my dear Spence, that you will find the most tactful way to put my services before the Honourable Company of Adventurers. Perhaps an honorarium of, shall we say, five hundred pounds. . . .

The sigh built to an outcry of horror and disgust.

"Order. Order." The judge's voice was hard and cold. Whistler's knuckles on the railing of the dock were bone-white.

Maître Gelinas raised his voice. "I put it to you, Harold Barker Whistler. Answer yes or no. Did you or did you not write that letter?"

The room fell silent. Whistler's easy bearing, his calm self-assurance, all collapsed. He seemed to fold and shrivel. His contemptuous mouth melted to a petulant circle. His lips began to quiver. No words came.

"Well, sir? Did you? Answer yes or no."

"I. . .I. . .I. . . Yes, I did." He sank slowly to his knees and his head dropped on his hands. His whole frame began to shake.

Duncan watched him as the noise in the courtroom grew. He could raise no more feeling towards Harry Whistler than he could for a fly. His own letter proved his guilt. So the Wolverine would die. And Duncan Cameron, Cut Hand's grandson, had tracked him down and seen that it was so. He took his pistol from inside his coat and emptied the powder from the pan.

Even greater, another thing shone crystal clear. Angus Cameron had not betrayed his wife. He had read last winter that Rose Flower and young Malcolm had died a tragic death. He honestly believed that she was dead. Whatever may have happened since, he had never turned his back. He had never turned his family off.

The courtroom emptied and was quiet at last. Angus Cameron sat at the counsels' table, facing his eldest son. He had one arm around Sally, the other around Raymond. A shaft of late-afternoon sun slanted through the tall window and lay along the polished surface. It lit the letters up so brightly you could scarcely read the words.

"Aye. Magnus Spence is a staunch and good friend," Cameron said. "He came to me the first moment that he could. And it's a long hard trip in winter. Then he stayed until I could travel with him to London. We decided to put the matter to the governors of the Bay in case Whistler came back to England. I couldna move for a time, you see, after the surgeons had finished."

"Did they sew you up properly?" Raymond whispered.

"What's that, wee Raymond? Och, aye. You can see the scar tonight, I promise."

He pushed Whistler's letter across the table to Duncan. It said a great deal more than had been read in court.

> . . .but, my dear Spence, I regret to tell you you sired a vixen. Our arrangement whereby I was to take your Nancy to wife and also care for your woman Jane and her younger child has broken down due to Nancy's outright viciousness. She has proved completely unwilling to 'love, honour and obey.' I know there are no church vows involved, but that's the minimum one must expect. All this in spite of generosity, persuasion, even firm discipline.

I cannot blame you, my dear fellow. It is the Indian side of her nature that has come completely to the fore. But I will, of course, require a modest annual stipend from you to care for Jane, as I'm without the solace of a young wife. Sad, is it not, that half-breed children so often are a disappointment?. . .

Frog Portage. So Whistler had already tried to break Nancy's spirit by that time. But when had they gone their separate ways? Where was she now? There were two people he could ask. He looked up. His father was waiting for him to finish reading.

"Duncan, Magnus Spence charged me to find some good man to take care of Jane, and to arrange a marriage for Nancy. And he's provided decent dowries for them both. He'd already given a good big sum to Whistler. The man's nearly in the poorhouse."

"Why doesn't he send for them instead?" Duncan asked.

"I offered to put up the money. But he really believes they'll all be happier where they are. In his way, you know, Magnus loves his family very much."

The decent bumbling poor old man. Duncan slowly shook his head. To live out the end of his life alone, not understanding how much love his own family had for him.

Sally said, "Father, I. . .we. . . When will we

256

meet your new wife?" She was looking up at him, biting her lip.

"New wife? Did you hear that from Letellier?"

"No, Marianne told me." There was agony in Sally's eyes.

"Well, there was this lady. . ." Cameron waved his hand. "After I heard your mother had died. A very winsome widow, Sally, wi' two young children of her own. And, well. . .I felt. . ."

"I understand, Father. You were right." Sally nodded. Tears coursed down her cheeks.

"Oh, Sally, Sally, you didn't know it ended?"

She shook her head. Her lips were trembling.

"Bonnie Sally. . ." He looked down at her for a time, then nodded slowly as though he'd just remembered something important. "You see, I had one wee condition." A smile crept to his lips. "I said she must accept my children as her own."

Duncan saw the lines soften in his father's face. He saw him pull his two young children close. He watched him bend and kiss each of them on their dark, glossy heads. One hand reached out across the table and gripped his own.

He heard him say, "But she would not agree."

Then Duncan saw something that he thought he never, ever would. Tears filled his father's eyes.

22
A Breed Apart

There was a nip in the air and the fields were white with frost when Duncan rode down to Saint-Sulpice to see the old Tremblays. Warm in their tidy little kitchen, he told them all he could about Ti'moine — his wife and children, his happy industrious life, his dogs, his singing, his solid loyal service. He spoke of their own friendship and finally his shocking sudden death. He didn't spare himself, and they were grateful.

They shared their own memories of the faithful son they hadn't seen for years. They declined Duncan's offer of money with quiet dignity. Any pension for their son, they said, should go to the widow and the children. When he said good-bye, though, he went to see the parish priest. It was arranged that he would hear should the Tremblays suffer any want.

Then at the Letelliers' there had been a celebration. The dining room gleamed with polished wood and silver, crystal and a hundred candles. It glittered with the elegance of evening dress. It warmed to a crackling fire and good friendships. Going in to find their places, Fergus Macdonald laid his arm over Duncan's shoulder. He growled in his ear, "A man should know who his friends are, Duncan — and who are not. I must tell ye, it was old MacGillivray voted down your licence at the council."

"Wee Willie was behind that, I suppose." Duncan laughed a little. It didn't surprise him. Oddly, it didn't bother him either. "Twelve years to get back at me for a bloody nose! Now that'll be the end of it."

Later Fergus Macdonald stood and raised his glass across the table. "I voted against your licence last year, Duncan, and I voted for it this summer. I want ye to know now that I'm with ye every time." He turned. "Angus Cameron, my friend, your son set one foot dead wrong. And ye were right to turf him out. But he's a man, I can tell ye that. He's proved it. And anyone who'll paddle and carry from Frog Portage to Fort William as a common canoeman for just his pride has good Highland blood in his veins. And good Cree blood too." He looked around the polished table at their friends. "He gets the same thing in good measure from his father and his grandfather both — and I've known the two for many years. Brown, white, half and half — I dinna care. He's a gentleman, I tell ye. And a true gentleman is hard to find."

Across the table Sally's eyes shone with joy in her father and them all. Angus Cameron had admitted to them his health would not stand more living in the northwest. He had sent an express to Dawson at Rapid River to ask Rose Flower to come down and join them with Cat and wee Malcolm in the spring. He'd be at Fort William to meet them. He had already looked at a fine estate on the river near Sainte-Anne.

Raymond, a miniature adult in his new suit, wrestled manfully with his knife and fork. He would quickly learn the ways of his new life — as quickly as he had begun to learn to trap with Cut Hand. He too would have to make up his own mind about so many things. . . .

"I'll make you an offer, Duncan." Raymond Letellier's smile was warm and open. "Assistant to my chief clerk, and you get his position when he retires in a couple of years."

And then a partnership. That was almost certain.

Marianne sat next to Duncan, and her voice led the chorus of approval. She sparkled. Her lovely oval face, her smile, bare shoulders, a touch of perfume, jewels. Her hand found his beneath the table and their fingers interlaced.

Duncan looked into her eyes for a steady moment. She loved life, did Marianne, and she would live it to the full. But at her own pleasure. He put her hand back in her lap. He smiled at her and shook his head. Then he turned to Raymond Letellier.

"Thank you again, sir. But I don't think I fit a Montreal bureau. I'd ask you to consider Gavin

Farquhar, though. You know how bright he is, Father. And you know how loyal. He stuck by me at Ile-à-la-Crosse when I had no other friend. Gavin would never let you down, sir. Never."

Now he had just one more call to make.

The cells beneath the courthouse were dank and chill. He followed the bent old turnkey along the rough-flagged passage. It was dimly lit, with rushlights hanging on the dripping walls. There was some stirring in the cells as they went by. Here a pale face showed at a tiny slot, there a pair of glittering eyes.

"Not the prettiest place, m'sieu. Too many prisoners since the old jail burned. That Whistler, though, he'll be gone tomorrow, for sure. I see the gallows ready. Room for one more at the inn then, eh, m'sieu?"

The turnkey cackled, and his shoulders heaved as he coughed. "It's the damp. The damp. Here he is, m'sieu. You wish for me to open the door?"

"Yes, please. And where's Pinet?"

The old man jerked his thumb at the opposite cell and sorted through the big keys on his ring. Duncan turned, and there were Pinet's eyes at the slot in the massive door.

"M'sieu Cameron," his voice rasped. "Please, m'sieu. . ."

Duncan turned his back and faced the black rectangle of the doorway into Whistler's cell.

The turnkey held his lantern up and stood back to let him in. He could just see the man sitting on the edge of the cot.

"I've nothing this side of hell to say to you, you brown bastard." Whistler spat straight at Duncan. He was unshaven, his face sunken, his eyes wild.

"Like your namesake, Wolverine, you never give an inch, even when your time's run out. I can't offer you a thing. I have some help for Jane Spence and her family, though. If you can tell me where she is, and Nancy. . ."

"Bitch!" Whistler spat again. "You're all alike, you. . .goddamned half-breeds. . ."

He leaped, made a lunge for Duncan's throat. Duncan stepped back, grabbed both wrists and tugged them downwards. He threw him against the wall. Whistler gave a gasp of pain and held one shoulder. His mouth clamped tight and his eyes glittered like a rat's. Liquor smelled on his breath.

Nothing could be pried from Harry Whistler. He had nothing left in him but hate, and rum to numb his final hours. Duncan stepped outside. The turnkey slammed the door.

"Heh, m'sieu. Heh." Pinet's voice came from the other side. "Me, I can tell you something. You'll help me, eh? Five years in jail. . . ."

Duncan turned towards his tiny slot. "At least they're not hanging you, crapaud. What is it you have to tell?"

"You want to know about that girl."

"Yes, Coco, I do. Tell me where I can find her."

"You'll get me off, m'sieu?" he whined. "A word from you. . . You promise?"

Duncan's heart began to beat more quickly. He kept his voice controlled and harsh. "No promises, Pinet. Just tell me where. Maybe you'll get some time off. If you lie, I swear I'll see you in jail for life."

"Oui, m'sieu. Where she is now, I don't know. But she got away at Sturgeon Lake."

"Got away?" Duncan moved closer. "What do you mean?"

"Well, m'sieu. She never goes with him, you know what I mean? She fights him off. After the fire at Hunter Bay there, she got a knife. She tried to kill him. He beat her so she can hardly walk. We carry her at the portages, like a pack of furs."

"Pinet, she was in his tent at Medicine Rapid."

"On an ankle chain."

"Ankle chain!"

"Since Lac la Ronge he keeps her on a chain. Until she shoots him."

"Shoots him?" Duncan's voice rang off the walls. He thrust his face to the slot, looked straight into Pinet's desperate eyes. "When? Where?"

"At Medicine Rapid, m'sieu. Of course, you must know that. Right there by the tent." His eyes shifted, narrowed. "Aha! Your back was turned. I remember."

263

And Duncan remembered. . .Whistler holding Nancy, a pistol in his hand. Noise behind. He whirled about.

"She snatched Whistler's pistol and shot him," Pinet raced on. "She only hit his shoulder, but then you got away."

"In the shoulder," Duncan breathed. "That's why I had no trouble with him over there?" He glanced back at Whistler's cell.

"That's right, m'sieu. And his arm's no good to paddle or to carry. Coco here does all the work."

And that's why that animal couldn't aim his pistol back in rue Saint-Louis. She had shot Whistler. If it hadn't been for that. . . Oh, God, why had he always thought the worst? What had he done? What had he thrown away?

"If he wasn't hurt so bad. . . Well, even Isbister kept his gun and knife away so he couldn't kill her. Then at Sturgeon Lake she got away."

"At Sturgeon Lake. Before the freeze?" The map was in Duncan's mind. Where would she go from there? Where could she be now?

"Oui, m'sieu. And he is mad with rage and drinks rum for the pain in his shoulder. Whistler thinks Isbister let her go. That's why he killed him."

There was a snarling curse from across the way. Whistler's face was at the slot. "Damn you, Pinet. Damn you, Cameron. Damn your eyes. Damn you to hell!" The voice began to rise. "That bitch. . . The two of you. . . ."

Would she ever. . .could she ever?. . . . Something stirred in Duncan's memory. He turned back.

"Pinet, when did you see her last?"

"At Sturgeon Lake, just like I said."

"What did she wear?"

"Wear, m'sieu? Blouse, black skirt, leggings, a capote."

"Around her neck?" Duncan almost held his breath.

"Around her neck? Oh, what she always wears, m'sieu. She never takes it off. That little silver tortue on the string. You know. What you call a turtle?"

"Thank you, Coco. You wretched toad, I thank you very much." That Sunday morning on the lake. The dogs, Ti'moine's toboggan. The silver turtle gleaming in the sun. Scratching their initials on it with his knife. Hanging it around her neck. . . .

He found some coins in his pocket, shoved them through Pinet's slot. "You can buy drink, Coco, or save some to buy a mass for yourself when you die. God knows, you'll need it. But I'll try my level best to get your time reduced."

Whistler shouted something and his voice cracked. Then it began to fill the low-ceilinged passage. He was screeching filth at Duncan, Pinet, Nancy, Isbister, Magnus Spence, the world. Duncan turned and walked back towards the stairs.

He came up from the stench of the cells. He

265

walked through the gleaming corridor, the big, high-ceilinged room with desks and cabinets, the ordered bustling of well-dressed clerks. He opened the stately door and stood on the steps among the city's sounds and smells. Above the mountain in the clear-washed sky, pristine clouds marched grandly from the west.

The geese were up there too. The first flight of the season, going south. He heard their urgent calling, as the old ones led their young on their first wondrous journey from the north. They would go back. And back again. And the young would learn the way themselves, and they would pass it on and on and on.

He looked down at the glengarry in his hand. With his finger he traced the ordered endless lines of beads. Scot. Cree. He could never have been both. And now he knew he really could be neither. But he was something else. He was a breed apart. He was himself.

Then he lifted his head and he laughed as he had not done since that sparkling day gliding along the frozen lake with her. And his laughter rose as it had then, unfettered, to the giant sky.

There to the northwest, somewhere, was Nancy Spence. He owed her his life. He owed her his love. Now that he had found himself, he would find her.

Glossary

The day-to-day language of the fur trade was French, but Indian and English words were freely mixed in.

ARMOIRE: wardrobe.

AU REVOIR: so long; good-bye for now.

AVANT: the bow paddler. In a large canoe, the most experienced paddler was stationed in the bow, where he had the best view ahead.

BABICHE: thongs made from hide and used for laces, snowshoes, etc.

BEAVER CLUB: an exclusive Montreal social club founded by partners of the North West Company in 1785 and famous for its carousing and lavish all-night dinner parties. Eligibility for membership required at least one winter in the northwest.

BELLE: beautiful; a beauty.

BIEN OUI: why, certainly.

BIENVENU: welcome.

BONJOUR, B'JOUR: good morning; good day.

BOURGEOIS: the clerk in charge of a canoe brigade or a post. A company partner. The boss. *Le grand bourgeois* was the "big boss," in charge of a district.

BRIGADE: a flotilla of perhaps a dozen trade canoes or York boats travelling together. Also referred to trains of wagons, pack horses or dog sleds.

CANADA JURISDICTION ACT: Intense competition between different interests from Montreal, as well as with the Hudson's Bay Company, brought lawlessness and violence to the fur trade, and in 1803 the British Parliament passed this Act empowering the Governor of Lower Canada to nominate Justices of the Peace for the Indian Territories.

CANOE: They varied in size from eight-foot hunting canoes to the big six-fathom (36-foot) *canot de maître* used between Montreal and the Lakehead. Its cargo consisted of sixty-five 90-pound *pièces*, and the crew averaged eight to ten. The four-fathom *canot du nord* was used in the northwest where waters were more restricted.

CALÈCHE: a two-wheeled carriage with a folding top.

CALUMET: a long ceremonial pipe. Smoking it together symbolized peace.

CANAILLE: scum; rogue.

CAPOTE: a hooded coat, usually made of blanket or duffle and tied with a sash.

CARRIOLE: a toboggan-shaped dog sled. The frame, built to contain the load or carry a passenger, was covered with parchment skin and often handsomely decorated. Today the canvas cargo-container on a dog sled is often called the "carryall."

CASSETTE: a light waterproof box with a lock, for carrying personal effects and valuables.

CHAW: to a sled dog — "go left." "Gee" means right. Other words were used in different areas. Skilful cracking of a whip to one side of the lead dog's head directs the team the opposite way. "Marche" means get up and go. The French word was converted by English speakers to "mush."

CHEZ NOUS: our place; our home.

CRAPAUD: toad.

CROOKED KNIFE: a short knife, bent to a curve, used as a draw knife for shaping wood. An axe, an awl and a crooked knife were the only tools needed to build any size canoe.

CUL-DE-SAC: dead end.

DÉCHARGER: to unload. *Un décharge* was a rapid which could be negotiated by carrying the load and lining, poling or running the lightened canoe.

EN DEROUINE: going out from the company's post and travelling around the Indian camps to trade and bring in furs.

ENGAGÉ: a fur company employee.

EXPRESS: The winter express was carried by dog sled in successive laps. Mail and fur returns leaving the Athabasca country in January would arrive at Sault Ste. Marie about April and then go on by express canoe to Montreal. An express canoe, carrying important mail or special passengers, would have a bigger crew and carry a light load.

FRIPON: rascal.

FAIT BEAU: "nice day."

FAMILLE: family.

FEMME DE BOURGEOIS: the boss's wife.

FEU DE JOIE: ceremonial firing of muskets or rifles in rapid succession.

FROG PORTAGE: The name comes from the story that some Cree Indians displayed a frog skin stretched in the manner of a beaver. This was to mock the ineptitude of their enemies, the Chipewyans, in hunting beaver and treating their skins and to warn them off. Benjamin and Joseph Frobisher and Louis Primeau from Montreal set up there in 1774 with trade goods, and intercepted the Cree who were on their annual trading trip to Fort Prince of Wales (Churchill) on Hudson Bay. This marked the start of fierce competition between the Hudson's Bay Company and "the pedlars from Montreal." Because of that historic event the place was also called *Portage de la Traite*.

LES GARS: the guys.

GIGUE: a jig.

GUIDE: as well as being the expert on the route, the rapids and the portages, the guide was in direct charge of the canoemen. He answered to the *bourgeois* for theft or loss, and the canoemen answered to him for their wages.

GLACIÈRE: an ice-house or pit for preserving meat.

GORGET: originally a piece of armour to protect the throat, it evolved into an ornamental silver crescent, worn by officers around their necks. Gorgets were valued items of trade silver and often given to leading Indians.

GOUVERNAIL: literally "rudder." The paddler in the

269

stern of a canoe. He was highly skilled and experienced. Like the *avant*, he wielded a seven-to-nine-foot paddle and he was paid double wages.

HOMME DU NORD: one who lived and worked in the fur trade west of the Great Lakes. They looked with disdain on the lesser men who travelled no further than the Lakehead.

HUNCH-CUDDY-HUNCH: a hurly-burly game played by all ages, and going by various names. The members of one team bend over in line, each clutching the legs of the person ahead. The other team members run from behind and leap in quick succession on their backs, trying to collapse the line before one of their own team falls off.

ILE-A-LA-CROSSE: The peninsula, which was almost an island, got its name from the tradition that Indians played lacrosse there during their summer gatherings. The Frobishers were trading there in 1776. The Hudson's Bay Company followed. The Hudson's Bay fort was burned by the Canadians in 1808 (in somewhat different circumstances from this story), rebuilt, then seized again in 1817. The violence only ceased with the amalgamation of the two companies in 1821.

LOBSTICK or LOB-PINE: trees at key points were conspicuously lobbed of their lower branches to mark the route.

MANGEUR DE LARD: "pork eater"; the derisive name given by the elite *hommes du nord* to the *voyageurs* who paddled the mere thousand miles from Montreal to the Lakehead. Their diet consisted of dried peas, beans or corn, sea-biscuit and fat pork.

MAUDIT: damned.

MILIEU: the lowest grade of canoeman, who paddled amidships, simply providing the power.

MISSINIPPE: the Indian name for the great river which rises in northwestern Saskatchewan and flows eight hundred miles to Churchill on Hudson Bay. In the early fur trade days it was known as the Englishman's River and is now called the Churchill.

MON AMI: my friend.

PADDLE: Basswood was a favourite material, stronger than spruce or pine, lighter than birch or maple. The *milieux*, who sat close to the water and provided power only, used short paddles about four feet long. The *avant* and *gouvernail* needed more purchase. Their paddles were seven to nine feet long.

PAQUETON: a back pack. *Engagés* were allowed to bring out a strictly limited *paqueton* of furs for trading on their own account.

PARCHMENT: skin (usually beaver) with the fur removed, then dried, was translucent and was used for windows and other utility purposes, such as the sides of *carrioles*.

PAS PROBLÈME: (*pas de problème*) no problem.

PAYS D'EN HAUT: up-country; the northwest.

PEMMICAN: meat (most often buffalo), dried, pounded fine, mixed with melted fat and often saskatoon berries, then sewn into ninety-pound skin *taureaux*. It kept well and was the highly nourishing, staple food of the fur trade.

PIÈCE: a pack. Trade goods and furs were tightly made up in ninety-pound canvas packages, stitched up and tied. Each *voyageur* was responsible for carrying six of these at a portage. He would sling one on his back with his tumpline, toss another on top and run off at a shuffling dog-trot. This meant three trips across the portage for each man.

PORTAGE: a carrying place; to carry across a portage. To prevent damage, the canoe was loaded and unloaded in the water, and held carefully away from rocks or roots. As each man had to take three loads across and the canoe had to be carried, canoemen would paddle some distance out of their way or take risks at a rapid to avoid portaging.

QUI PASSE?: a sentry's challenge — "who goes there?"

QUOI?: what?

REGALE: a ration of liquor all round to celebrate a special event.

271

RUB-A-BOO: pemmican boiled up with flour and anything else available to make a tasty stew.

SACREMENT!: damn!

SPANISH DOLLAR: There was very little English coinage about, and Spanish silver dollars were widely used in North America.

STICK FISH: In the cool fall weather, fish are hung on sticks thrust through their gills and dried for winter dog food.

STRATHSPEY: a rhythmic Scottish dance, to rather slow-paced music.

SOU: (or *sol*) a French regime coin worth about a penny.

TANTE: aunt.

TORTUE: turtle. Silver turtles were popular trade items.

TUMPLINE: a strap, widened in the middle to go around the forehead, used to haul a toboggan, track a canoe or carry a heavy pack.

TURLINGTON'S BALSAM OF LIFE: a patent medicine, given the King's Royal patent in 1744, and still being sold in the late nineteenth century. It claimed to cure all manner of ailments including "stone, colic and inward weakness," and probably did contain some beneficial ingredients.

VIOLONISTE: violinist; fiddler.

VOYAGEUR: a canoeman of any grade.

WATAPE: split roots, usually spruce, used to sew bark in canoe building, etc.

WENDIGO: an evil man-eating spirit; one who has resorted to cannibalism and become possessed of an evil spirit with an insatiable appetite for human flesh.

WISKEDJAK: (various spellings). The mischief-maker in Indian mythology, who often takes the shape of a raven. Adapted to "whiskyjack," it refers to the cheeky grey jay.